SMOOTH

SMOOTH
EROTIC STORIES FOR WOMEN

EDITED BY
RACHEL KRAMER BUSSEL

CLEIS
PRESS

Published in the United States by Cleis Press, Inc., 2246 Sixth Street, Berkeley, California 94710.

Printed in the United States.
Cover design: Scott Idleman
Cover photograph: Alain Daussin/Getty Images
Text design: Frank Wiedemann
Cleis Press logo art: Juana Alicia
First Edition.
10 9 8 7 6 5 4 3 2 1

ISBN: 978-1-57344-408-8

Contents

INTRODUCTION: NAKED GIRLS IN ALL THEIR GLORY

*S*mooth. *Sleek. Naked. Bare.* All of these words describe the women you'll find in this book, women who let you peek beneath their skirt hems, unbutton their blouses, reach inside their panties and in so doing, reveal something essential about themselves. They aren't content to simply let sex happen but are compelled to explore the ways their bodies react to every tactile moment.

These are not stories about body image or learning to love your curves. These are sensual tales in which women and men celebrate the joy of being carnal, lusty, hungry and animalistic; stories in which the urge to get naked, in the literal and figurative senses, drives women to boldly go where they haven't before.

In the opening story, the stunning sauna romp "Löyly," by Angela Caperton, Sorrow Cove becomes a very happy place when our heroine, Andie, submits to a sensual beating in the intense heat. Caperton writes, "Blood pounded in my veins and pooled suspiciously in my belly. Anticipation added an edge of tension and vulnerability before the bright shock of the strike. It wasn't hard, but the leaves laced my skin with firm control, a lush wetness and a shimmer of sting that slashed my back with an awakening charge of delight. I closed my eyes, savoring the moment, the fresh scent of the birch binding me in a cloud of awareness and newfound sensation."

Food and sex are clearly twin appetites waiting to be released, and in "The Sushi Girl," by Anika Gupta, they converge in a work setting for the narrator as she balances raw fish on her body. She doesn't just lie there, though; she engages with her customers, lets them look and taste even as she makes sure her naked body, while still, speaks loudly.

Each of these women are stripped, whether literally, as in Clancy Nacht's story of the same name, or in some other way that leaves them vulnerable, exposed, open to whoever they've let enter their most personal space. Even when they are acting as voyeurs, watching others strip down, as in "Live Action," by Susan St. Aubin, they are being changed by what they see, by the skin that speaks to them and their fantasies.

For other characters, adorning their bodies—with tattoos in "Ink," by Jennifer Peters, or the sensual strokes of a paintbrush in "True Colors," by Louisa Harte—is a way to live a more vibrant, outspoken life, and their reward is a richer sex life than they'd had before. That makes sense, because when we bare all, we invite others to touch, to feel every curve, every bend, every inch of skin.

Ultimately, this is a book about getting to know your body from the outside in, about showing yourself off for a lover and knowing the power the naked body holds. At the gym, in the shower, on the subway, at a tea party, the women in *Smooth* leave behind their inhibitions and go where many women have only dreamed about. Sexy, playful, sensual and celebratory, these nineteen stories will be sure to entice you as they reveal so much skin.

Rachel Kramer Bussel
New York City

LÖYLY

Angela Caperton

A lone, at the north end of nowhere, I looked out through the rented Equinox's windshield at the green roof of the hotel. Copper. Copper had been king in this part of Michigan a lifetime ago. In a more civilized place, the owners of the hotel might have to hire a private army to keep thieves from stripping the roof, but not out here—it was too far away from anything to warrant the attention of scavengers.

I really had lost my mind. What the fuck was I going to do at a snowbound resort on Lake Superior in fucking November? Damn you to hell, Jeff. "Best snowmobiling in the country! You'll love it!"

"You'll love it," I mimicked as I clutched the steering wheel and contemplated spinning out of the driveway and hauling ass back to Savannah.

A young man—puppy, really—stepped smartly down the wide steps that led to a wide wraparound porch. His navy blue parka was unzipped, the hotel logo shining gold on the right shoulder. He walked around the front of the SUV and opened the driver's door.

"Welcome to Sorrow Cove!" He puffed mist and the blast of cold air that slapped me in the face nearly killed me. I shut off the engine of the SUV, took the keys and my purse and exited the car.

The young man efficiently scribbled information on a claim ticket and I handed him the keys.

"Your name, miss?" he asked as he made notes on the ticket.

"Andie Fortner."

He nodded and handed me the claim ticket. "Your luggage in the back?"

"Yes."

"My name's Luke. I'll park your car and take your bags to your room, Miss Fortner. Enjoy your stay at Sorrow Cove." He grinned at me with genuine hospitality, and I found my cheeks cracking against the cold to return it.

"Thank you," I managed, hoping my dismay at my own idiocy didn't echo in the words.

He drove away. I stood for a moment in the gray slush of the driveway and stared up at the mammoth Queen Anne–style mansion, water dripping in a steady stream from its gutters. Snow covered every inch of the landscape, weighing down massive boughs of cedars and evergreens, topping winter-bare hedges and what I imagined were lush lawns in the summer.

Snow. Goddamn snow.

"Fuck," I said under my breath as I made my way into the hotel.

I stared at the dull mourning-gray ceiling of the spacious room. A deliciously soft bed cradled me in the warmth of my own body. I didn't want to move, didn't dare breach the cocoon I'd wrapped around myself. Jeff should have been there with me, his strong arms around me, his cock nudging my ass, a living alarm clock. He liked fucking in the mornings, liked working out the kinks with a ride or a suck. Bastard.

Why had I listened to Sonia? "Just go, honey! It's already paid for, I bet there aren't any refunds. Extending his contract in Riyadh was Jeff's choice—not yours."

No more. Jeff had blown me off more times than I could count, and this little vacation had been his idea, not mine. I pulled the covers over my head and spent the next several minutes envisioning Jeff being eaten by cannibals.

I groaned and shoved the covers away, letting the blast of morning air temper my resolve. I wasn't going to stay in bed and wallow. After all, Lake Superior was practically at my doorstep and I had made it this far. Within an hour I had showered, dressed and armed myself with a map, determination and a pocket full of credit cards. A little breakfast and I'd be ready to tackle anything.

Except a blizzard.

I stepped off the stairs into the lobby, dominated by wide bay windows that provided guests with a glorious view of the cove, the lake and the woods on the east side of the estate. This morning the view was monochromatic, swirling, thick white with whiter highlights battering the panes of glass. I ignored the ball of unease forming in my stomach and walked into the empty dining room, the massive fireplace on one end filling the room with warmth and the pleasant scent of burning wood. A young woman in tight jeans and a thick sweater smiled at me and motioned. "Please, have a seat. Can I get you coffee?"

"Black." I looked out the windows again and smiled. "Big."

I ate my breakfast in silence, watched a few couples come

and go, listened to the murmurs of quiet conversation and willed the snow to stop. I can handle a lot of things, but a big SUV in a whiteout was not one of them.

Full of coffee and breakfast, I made my way to the front desk. "Good morning, Ms. Fortner. How can I help you?"

"What can you tell me about the weather?"

The clerk's bald head nearly blushed. "The snow should slow by tomorrow."

"Slow?"

"Yes, we're in for a few days of it here, but tomorrow the snowmobiling and cross-country skiing should be excellent."

"I was hoping to do a little sightseeing actually, maybe some shopping."

He didn't laugh, didn't even smile, but I could feel his desire to do both. "The roads to town are closed right now, Ms. Fortner. They should be open tomorrow, once the plows come through."

I nodded as I envisioned myself holed up for days, only one room service tray away from hanging myself with shoelaces.

"My credit cards are safe for another day," I said sardonically.

"There's a game room to the left and a small gym and indoor pool behind the dining room. And the sauna. It's not in the main building, but you can get to it from the pool area, or from the hall exit. Just follow the walkway."

I looked out the windows at the endless falling wall of white. Sure. Just follow the walkway. My luck, I'd end up in Canada.

"Thank you," I said, and headed back up the stairs to my room, kicking myself in the ass all the way. I should have fucking held out for Martinique.

I'd been surprised by the pool, really. I knew from making the reservations that the resort had a pool, but I wasn't expecting a pool I could actually do laps in. Who knew the tundra tribe understood the needs of us South-Coasters. The heated water and condensation on the broad bay windows made me feel at home—except for the snow beyond, of course.

I swam for an hour, then I dragged my pruned body out of the pool, showered in the little changing room and stepped back out on the deck to stand transfixed by the vista beyond the foggy windows. While annoyed by the shitty weather, I loved the beauty and serenity of the snowfall. The large flakes drifted down completely at the whim of whatever wind might blow. Some fell heavy, wet, like obese calcified raindrops; others drifted to the ground in intricate Zen paths.

The perfect blanket over the ground amazed me. Painted green, the smoothness of the carpet would have been the envy of Augusta National.

Except for the quickly filling divots leading off into the veil. Footprints made not long ago, headed toward what?

The sauna. Someone apparently had a GPS and had found the temple of Sorrow Cove.

The grin started in my belly, and without a moment's analysis, I wrapped my robe around myself, scuffed on my rubber clogs and found the door leading outside. The blast of cold air almost made me run back to my room, but I had to do this—I had to beat the elements, had to take control of the vacation I'd never wanted but had inherited. If this trip was going to have any meaning, I needed to make it my own, not let it stay Jeff's irrelevancy.

The snow kissed my hair and clung to my robe, the cold air keeping it from melting right away. My breath sprayed in front of me like fueled smoke as I squinted against the snowfall to focus on the little shack, the destination of the quickly filling tracks.

When I reached the little building, I pulled the door open, praying I'd not find hedge trimmers and jugs of pesticide. My prayers were answered with a vision—glorious, living sculpture.

Rodin. Michelangelo.

Sculpted thighs; corded arms, pecs and abs; a brooding countenance.

And not one beautiful inch concealed by clothing.

"The door. You let the steam out."

Steam? Out? No, I thought as I let the closing door slap me in the butt. All the steam must be in here, boiling my blood, peaking my heartbeat. Surely I was producing enough heat now to replace any that had escaped in smoky plumes through the open door.

I was staring at his nakedness. "Oh, I'm sorry! I didn't realize—" I turned quickly, fumbling for the door latch.

"No, please stay." Not the Yooper accent of the locals. Dutch, maybe? "Welcome."

Beyond the door—snow and another gutter ball on the scorecard. I could do this. I had to do this.

I turned back around and smiled, feeling a little foolish as Adonis pulled a towel over his groin. Damn.

He jutted his chin toward the wall, and I saw a row of wooden pegs. A thick moss green robe hung from one of the pegs, and I quickly removed my own robe and hung it beside his.

The small room was completely made of wood—smooth slats of cedar covered the floor, the walls, the ceiling and the two-level bench. Adonis sat at one end of the lower bench beside what looked like a stove filled with large gray and brown rocks. A bucket of water sat at his feet.

He leaned over and dipped a ladle into the water and looked over his shoulder at me. "Sit," he nodded to the bench. I tried to look casual as I took a seat a comfortable distance from him and watched as he poured the water over the rocks.

Steam rose from the hot stones, quickly dissipating. Heat bloomed in the room and I found myself smiling.

Adonis sat back on the bench and looked at me. Small beads of sweat glistened on his upper lip. What would he do if I offered to lick the sweat off? He reached out a long-fingered hand. "I am Matias. Matias Toskala."

I grinned and gripped his hand in a polite shake. "Andie Fortner." Naked. Only a tenuous scrap of terry stood between us. "I'm really sorry about barging in. I didn't know," my voice trailed off as my cheeks burned.

"I was not expecting anyone else, but it is okay. Naked is best for sauna." He brushed long light brown bangs from his forehead.

"It is?" *Smooth, Andie.*

"Tradition. Back home, saunas are enjoyed bare, though not often men and women together."

"Where's home?"

"Helsinki, Finland. I teach at university and am here to lecture at the school in Hancock."

"I'd say you're a long way from home but considering the weather and the fact that we're in a sauna, I guess I'm the alien here." If my accent didn't scream Dixie draft, Dolly Parton would weep.

He laughed softly, his smile genuine and disarming. "Do you know about saunas?"

"I know they're hot, and make you sweat, but that's about all—oh, and that they are best experienced naked." I said with a grin.

Naked. He wasn't putting the moves on me, and he was comfortable with his own nakedness. What the hell? I'd dashed through a blizzard to reach this shack, and if a real live Finn was telling me naked was the way to go, well, tan lines be damned, naked was what I was going to be.

If my knees would hold me up.

I stood and slid the straps of my one-piece off my shoulders and in a momentary flood of courage, peeled the wet material off my body in one hopefully graceful movement. I waited for the high school marching band to burst through the doors and seal my embarrassment, but it didn't happen. Instead, the shock of my spontaneity melted like butter into an odd ease. I walked back over to the peg where my robe hung and deposited my suit. It was the turning back around and walking the two steps to my towel that seemed unreasonable.

With a deep breath and racing heart, I made that turn and took my seat again. I looked at Matias with a broad smile. He was watching me, all of me, but there was no leer in his eyes, just calm appraisal.

"So, naked's best. What else about saunas?"

His eyebrow quirked, but his face remained passive. He took up the ladle again and poured more water over the stones. There was a little mist, but the steam quickly filled the room with more heat. "That is *löyly*—steam—but it means more. *Löyly* is also spirit."

"The sauna has a spirit?"

"It can be said, yes." He poured another ladle over the rocks. As the heat washed over me, my bones turned to putty and every pore in my skin sighed.

I smiled. Better spirit than the bourbon I'd drunk the night before.

Matias moved his towel aside. I tried not to stare but his cock bounced attractively as he rose from his seat. Reaching to the wall, he took what appeared to be a small tree limb from its hook. On the long branches, bright green leaves shone with moisture. "This is a *vihta*—birch leaves. We beat the skin with the branches."

"Beat?"

He gave the gathered branches a little shake, then stretched across his opposite shoulder to swat his back. More attractive bouncing followed, and I really had to resist reaching out to touch him.

"They stimulate the skin," he said and held the branches out to me.

"Okay," I said without much conviction, but hey, in for a penny, in for a pound.

I tried to wrap my hand around the gathered stems, but the individual thin branches seemed determined to flop their own way in spite of the straw binding at the base.

He chuckled again and reached for the branches. "Here," he said, taking the *vihta* in a masterful hand that had the branches sliding into submission. He dipped the leaves into another bucket of water, then smiled at me. "Turn away, and pull your hair back. You will see."

See what? I wondered as I did as he said. Naked and alone with a naked man about to be flayed with a tree: I could see the postcard to my mother now.

Blood pounded in my veins and pooled suspiciously in my belly. Anticipation added an edge of tension and vulnerability before the bright shock of the strike. It wasn't hard, but the leaves laced my skin with firm control, a lush wetness and a shimmer of sting that slashed my back with an awakening charge of delight. I closed my eyes, savoring the moment, the fresh scent of the birch binding me in a cloud of awareness and newfound sensation.

The second strike layered the first, a few leaf tips stroking the backs of my arms and the nape of my exposed neck. The rich cream of arousal mixed with wonder as the birch blessed my skin. My back warmed further, the skin made new with the sharp, green kisses. My mind drifted, like it did after too much wine, and I arched like a cat, my back bowed to invite the next strike, the tender flesh over my ribs and sides of my breasts exposed.

Beads of perspiration and condensation trickled down my sides and under my breasts, and my pussy, exposed to the steam of the sauna, to this bizarre, otherworldly moment, swelled and slicked.

Every inch of my skin hummed with the heat and humidity of the sauna, and my mind became the fulcrum between my body and my soul. Desire coursed through me, my pussy anticipating the next strike of the birch with a heartbeat pulse that nearly melted me. My breath matched the rolling press of air, water and fire.

The next strike sliced my upper back, light nettles bolting sensation from the side of my right breast directly to the untouched nipple. I imagined Matias's teeth clamping on the nub, sucking at the nipple, cupping the weight and branding me with his tongue.

I needed his cock. I wanted him in the most savage, most basic way a man and woman could connect. I needed him to fuck me. He'd beaten me, after all. I willingly sat in this little hut of wet fire and let him strike me with sticks. His balls slapping my ass didn't seem a stretch.

I leaned far forward, my arms trembling, my breath a rush in my ears, and the birch fell again twice, rapidly, the second harder than the first and lashing just across the crack of my ass. Nerves raw, flayed to the feverish temperature of the sauna, I felt the last strike across the small of my back and the top of my ass and it tossed me to the edge of orgasm.

I moaned. I barely heard it above the ringing pulse in my ears, my lips, my pussy, but the sound rattled off the wood walls of the sauna.

I dripped from my nose, my arms, my chin, my sex. Every inch of me bloomed and reached, seeking yet full, as I plumped with liquid fire even as I was released, renewed, revived. Jeff's dismissal, my mundane job, the honest absurdity of my being in Michigan in November all faded comfortably into the realm of the inconsequential. All that mattered was the sure pulse of my blood, the heavy drop of my heart, the electric thrill of my nerves. Water collected on my skin, housed me, cleansed me, invigorated me, and I, for the first time in my life, felt everything.

The hiss of water on hot stones barely registered. I hungered for the blow; for the leaves to cut and slap my skin, my body, my being into frenzy, but only the sizzle of dying water greeted my ears.

Awkward, I settled back on my towel and looked over my shoulder at Matias. He smiled, polite and knowing, and his eyes, the shining mysterious green of sage, burned into me.

"So now you know some of the sauna," he said as he rose. "But nothing is good if too much. Best to see more at different times."

He moved, fluid and sure, to his robe hanging on the post. "It is time to go," he said over his shoulder. "Don't stay too long, Andie Fortner." He opened the door, the frozen air killed by the steam before it reached me, then the door closed and he was gone.

I flopped back on the bench. What the hell had I done wrong? My fingers drifted to my clit, but I could not bring myself to shatter the thrum that radiated through me.

I stayed another fifteen minutes, stretched on the low bench, bare as the moon and totally enraptured by the heat and humidity, even while I unsuccessfully willed Matias back into the shack.

Fuck. What? Did he only like blondes? Was it my accent? Did I drool too much while he was using the birch?

I managed to coagulate my limp muscles and bones and rose to don my robe. Rubber clogs in place, swimsuit stuffed into the robe pocket, I opened the door and bravely faced the blizzard. The shock of the cold invigorated me, but that didn't keep me from nearly running to the door of the pool.

Less than two minutes later I was in my room. The cottony warmth and artificial comfort were walls I wanted to blast apart.

I fell on the bed and closed my eyes, trying to filter what had just happened, trying to recapture the perfect freedom of the experience. In the span of thirty minutes, I had stripped to my skin in front of a man I didn't know, had talked to that man, had let him *beat* me with leaves and had...had...

The rap on my door nearly stopped my heart. I jolted off the bed, clutching the robe at my throat.

I pressed my ear to the door and spoke firmly. "Yes?"

Muffled but recognizable came a voice: "It's Matias."

Heat, the flush of unseen steam, gushed through me, tapped that illusive germ of my knowing and began the slow expanse of understanding I'd discovered in the sauna. I pressed my thighs together in hopes of stilling the blitz of desire that rapped my pussy with snare precision and sent my heart to wild trilling.

I opened the door, only half holding my robe closed and smiled at the handsome Finn, his long, dark blond bangs falling over his green eyes. He still wore his robe. Full lips curled in an almost sheepish grin. He leaned against the door frame and braised me with an openly lustful gaze.

"The sauna, you liked it?" he asked, his accent bronze and weighted. "You liked the *vihta*?"

Saliva pooled in my mouth, but I clutched the door like an unwanted defense. "I did, very much. I liked it more than I thought I would."

"Saunas, they are not for sex. For cleansing, for contemplation...for...opening." His face contorted as he seemed to struggle for words. He reached out and stroked my cheek, and the same hand that had held the clutch of birch traced my lips, my chin. Shivers of desire collected in my stomach.

I smiled and cupped his face in my hands. My robe opened and his warm hands took the opportunity to reach in and begin a slow exploration. "I may not know what saunas are for," I said, "but we both know what they can inspire. The question is, would the *löyly* approve?"

Matias's smile broke like dawn. He held up his strong right hand, the index and middle finger crossed. "Don't worry, Andie," he said with solemn assurance. "Me and the *löyly* are like that."

I reached under his robe. Oh, yes. Hot, carved marble. He crossed the threshold, gathered me in his arms. The touch of our lips sizzled, water on hot rocks, the steam a gift of spirit and will.

He stripped me, his hands rough and tender. He claimed all of me by the right he knew I had bequeathed him, by the power of what he had shown me. I licked the line of his jaw and his neck, tasting salt and delicious spice. My left hand trailed down his chest, across his abs and into the gold tangle at the base of his belly.

Silk-covered wood, long and hard. Oh, yes, beat me again. I held his cock in my hand, and he lengthened and hardened more. He pushed me back onto the bed. I spread open for him, beyond ready. That my pussy didn't shout orders like a drill sergeant amazed me.

His throaty chuckle conveyed his understanding. No ceremony—none needed—he thrust cleanly and deeply, filling me in one breath-stealing slide, making me whole. Firm, talented hands stroked and pulled, and his mouth met mine with heat that shamed the sauna. We gasped together, breath mingling, our skin becoming seamless, slicking with sweat where we touched. Electric, majestic, unstoppable, we rose together, vapor against the cold, rapture a promise in the match of souls.

I creamed, my greedy pussy filled with his slick cock and with the elixir of my orgasm. He ground into me, thrusting deep. He reached climax and stayed all the way in me as though he wanted to pierce my soul.

As bright ripples of orgasm bound us, we became the heat and the steam, and ecstasy became a divine gift of fire and water, body and soul.

In that moment, Matias and I, together we were the *löyly*.

HER BRAND-NEW SKIN

Elizabeth Coldwell

Don't let them talk you into staying at the villa, I thought as I listened to my husband's half of the phone conversation. *I know we really need a holiday, and it'll be lovely to see Bill and Laura again, but not there, not this year.*

"Great, so it's all settled," I heard Jon say. "I'll let Sarah know. I'm sure she'll be delighted." He put the phone down and turned to me. "We're sorted. Bill's just booked the villa for the third week in June. It's not too hot then, and it means we get out there before the schools break up."

I tried not to let my face fall. I didn't want him to see how disappointed I was by the decision. Holidaying with Bill and Laura had never been a problem before; we'd been friends with the couple for years, ever since Bill had become my husband's project manager at work. Even though they were both a good ten years older than us, we seemed to have more in common with them than most people our own age. I can't remember who first suggested we should all go on holiday together, but that year we spent a week at a villa in the south of France. Bill had found the place on the Internet, and it had been perfect: quiet and secluded, with the nearest neighbors half a mile down the road. We had spent the time lounging by the pool, the four of us so relaxed in each other's company that we had been happy to swim and sunbathe naked together, and the night before we were due to return to England, after dinner in a nearby restaurant and maybe one too many liqueur coffees, we had ended up swapping partners. Feeling Bill's thick cock thrusting up into me while I watched Jon eagerly lick Laura's pussy was one of the most exciting things I had ever done. None of us had any regrets as we traveled to the airport the following morning and, indeed, there was an unspoken feeling that if the circumstances were right, we would all be happy to do it again.

The next year, the villa wasn't available when all four of us were free, and so we settled on a break in Amsterdam, staying on a houseboat on one of the city's main canals. It soon became clear that we were all eager to repeat the fun and games we'd enjoyed the time before, but the slightly cramped confines of the boat didn't exactly lend themselves to sexual experimentation. Instead, we made our first ever visit to a swing club, though from the confident way Bill and Laura strode around the place wearing nothing more than tiny towels—which they both quickly discarded—I sensed that, unlike us, they weren't exactly new to the scene. Hand in hand with my husband, I wandered through the club, taking in the sight of so many combinations of lovers and reveling in the feeling of being an unashamed voyeur. Though I knew I could never pair off with a stranger, as so many of the women here were doing, I was more than happy to join Jon, Bill and Laura in one of the private playrooms for a foursome. I was aware that, as we fucked, people might be watching through the small, high windows designed for the purpose—but that only added to the thrill. In the company of our good friends, I was beginning to discover and enjoy a side of my sexuality I had never known existed.

We had vaguely started discussing where we might go the following year, when I had my accident. Walking home from the tube station on a wet weeknight, I was hit by a plumber's van that lost control and mounted the pavement. Most of my memories from that night are still a blank, but my injuries were so severe that I was in the hospital for a couple of months and needed a series of extensive skin grafts. The result was that I now had scars that ran from my right breast all the way down to my hip, and the skin on that side of my body had a strangely taut look to it that would never fully go away.

I supposed I was lucky; if the scarring had been on my face, I knew I would have been stared at in the street, and even people I had known for a long time would have looked at me differently without meaning to. At least I was able to hide what I couldn't help but think of as my disfigurement beneath my clothing.

But now Jon had agreed to our going on a holiday where everyone would more than likely take the opportunity to strip off completely—and I just couldn't do that anymore. Since I had finally come out of the hospital, I had been incredibly reluctant to let him see me naked, worried that he would find the sight of my scarred body a turnoff. To his eternal credit, he had been nothing but sympathetic. He had always loved to see me in seductive lingerie, and now he actively encouraged me to leave it on for sex, treating me to skimpy silk nighties and gorgeous velvet and lace basques that flattered my slender figure. He would dress me in stockings and suspenders and then spend ages kissing my stockinged feet before working his way up my legs, so that by the time his teasing tongue finally reached my pussy, I was frantic with impatience to be licked there. On the very rare occasions when I was naked as we fucked, I always made sure the lights were off and we were in the spooning position, so I could lie on my damaged side. It wasn't always entirely comfortable, but it kept Jon's roving hands away from the places I didn't want him to touch.

I hadn't explained any of this to anyone else; I had never really needed to, as I had never been one for dressing in low-cut or midriff-revealing tops, even before the accident. But holidays were different. Bill and Laura would quickly notice that I had traded in my usual bikini for…for what? A one-piece would have to be chosen very carefully, so that it didn't draw attention to any of the scarring. Otherwise, I could just sink into middle age about twenty years before my time and settle for one of those unflattering floral kaftans they sell in the back pages of the Sunday supplements.

It was all so silly. It wasn't as though either of our friends possessed a perfect centerfold body. Bill had one of those cocks that is barely there when it's limp and seems to come surging out of nowhere to full hardness, while Laura's breasts were heavy and pendulous and she had a little round tummy that never went away no matter how hard she exercised, and yet they were both completely comfortable with their naked state. That was what had changed. I was no longer comfortable in my own skin: though the surgeons had worked so skillfully to patch me up, my body didn't feel like mine anymore. Perhaps it never would.

I thought I had managed to keep my expression neutral, but Jon knows me far too well for that. "You are okay with this, aren't you, Sarah?" he asked.

"I'm sure we'll have a good time," I replied, "but…well, I'm worried about Bob and Laura seeing my scars. I just don't think I can go naked anymore, and I don't want them to think I've turned into some kind of prude."

"They'll never think that of you, love," he assured me, giving me a hug. "Don't worry. This could turn out to be the best holiday you've ever had."

The French sun was hot on the back of my neck as we got out of the taxi. It was late afternoon, and the villa seemed to bask in the heat, fat bumblebees suckling in the hibiscus flowers that grew round the doorway.

Laura wheeled her case behind her as she walked up the path. "This place hasn't changed a bit," she said, her tone excited. "God, I can't wait to strip off and dive into the pool."

"Sounds like an idea," Bob agreed, stuffing his wallet back into his pocket after paying the taxi driver. "Let's dump the luggage and then we'll go for a swim. Jon, the owners said they'd stock the fridge for us—can you check if they put a bottle of fizz in there, like I asked? You going to join us in the pool, Sarah?"

"Just let me settle in a little first," I said, "and then I'll be with you."

I took my time unpacking, before changing into the navy blue and white tankini I'd bought for the trip. It seemed like the best compromise, being just fashionable enough as swimwear while carefully concealing my torso. However, I wasn't surprised that by the time I wandered out to join the others, Laura was lying topless on one of the sun loungers while Bob, in nothing but a pair of baggy trunks, was smoothing SPF 15 into her freckly Celtic skin. A shirtless Jon was pouring champagne into glasses. He smiled at me as I joined them.

"Sarah, that looks great on you," he said, handing me a glass.

"Yes, very Brigitte Bardot," Bob added, giving me an approving look. "Nautical but nice."

So I had passed the first hurdle; no one had commented on

the fact I was relatively covered up compared to the rest of
them, and Bob was paying me as many outrageous compliments
as he always had. I'd always known Bob was a bit of a lech,
but in such an inoffensive fashion that no one could ever be
upset by him.

Relishing the bite of the champagne bubbles on my tongue,
I lay back on my lounger and enjoyed that glorious moment
when your body registers that you're actually on holiday and
begins to relax. I watched through half-closed eyes while the
other three splashed around in the pool, Laura shrieking with
mock-horrified laughter as Bob dove under the water and pulled
down her bikini bottoms. I envied their lack of self-conscious-
ness, but no one paid too much attention to the fact that I stayed
where I was, still covered up, still with no inclination to dive into
the water and join in their horseplay. Bob and Laura knew all
about my accident; even if they didn't know quite how deeply it
had affected me—and continued to do so—it seemed they were
prepared to give me some leeway.

And if I was honest, I was quite enjoying the sight of them all
having fun. I never grew tired of looking at Jon's body, trim and
compact, with a cock that looked as appetizing in its relaxed
state as it did when it was erect, and watching our friends
groping and tickling each other was starting to make my pussy
moisten. I had the urge to drag Jon into our bedroom and fuck
him right there, with the sunlight streaming through the blinds.
I reckoned I'd look quite cute in just my tankini top, my bottom
raised up and thrusting back at Jon as he plowed into me from
behind. And then Bob yelled at me, asking whether there was
any champagne left in the bottle, and the moment passed.

Jon clambered out of the pool. "You okay there?" he asked,
putting a wet hand on my thigh. I nodded, and his hand moved
up my body, rucking up my top to bare a little of my stomach.

I stopped him there. "Not yet, Jon," I whispered. "I'm not ready yet."

For the next couple of days I still wasn't ready. I pottered around the villa in a floaty sundress, or a vest top and shorts, while Laura wore little more than a smile, but no one made any mention of the fact they she was working on an all-over tan while I was still pretty much fully dressed.

In the evening, we would usually walk down the road into the village for dinner, lingering over coffee until we were the only people in the place. Laura claimed she enjoyed the novelty of having someone cook for her, even though Bob told us she never did anything more ambitious than pour a jar of sauce over chicken breasts and stuff them in the oven when she got in from work. In contrast, I loved to show off my culinary skills; while I had been at home, recuperating, I had grown much more imaginative in my choice of recipe, and one night I decided that instead of eating out, I would make dinner for everyone.

I spent the morning shopping in the local market, buying all the ingredients for a classic French bouillabaisse, along with plenty of salad vegetables, crisp baguettes and cheese so ripe and runny it could probably have made its way home ahead of me. Bob, who prided himself on his knowledge of wine, acquired a couple of bottles of merlot and more champagne to accompany the feast.

Jon popped into the kitchen a couple of times while I was preparing everything, savoring the rich aromas of garlic, tomato and gently simmering seafood. "That smells fantastic," he said. "I think tonight is going to be a very special evening."

I paused in the act of cracking eggs for the rouille that would accompany the fish stew. The last time the words "very special evening" had been used was in Amsterdam, before the four of us had visited the swing club. It was hard to deny that the prospect of a little adventure had been bubbling away beneath the surface ever since we had first arrived here. The way Jon would apply lotion to Laura's thighs, his fingers almost accidentally brushing the crotch of her bikini bottoms, or the expression on Bob's face as he watched me dangling my pink-polished toes in the pool made that obvious. At some point before the week was over, we were going to have another foursome, and though part of me was more than ready for it, I still wondered how it would ever happen if I wasn't prepared to get naked.

"If I'd known sex was on the agenda, I'd have cooked something with less garlic," I quipped.

Jon wrapped his arms round me, and I felt his cock resting in the groove between the cheeks of my bottom. "You're having a good time here, aren't you?"

"Yes," I assured him. "It's so nice just to be able to forget about everything. Well, nearly everything."

"Don't worry," he said. "No one's going to make you do anything you don't want to."

"Oh, I want to all right." I put my wooden spoon to Jon's lips so he could taste a little of the rich, aromatic sauce. "Do you think the others will like it?"

"Like it? They'll love it," Jon replied, and then he went back to the pool to join them, leaving me to wonder whether he was really talking about the meal.

We ate on the terrace, the last of the day's heat beginning to seep away as we looked out over the pool and the flower garden beyond it. I don't know whether I'd had it in the back of my mind when I chose the dish, but the classic way of eating bouillabaisse is to scoop it up on slices of bread and top it with a dollop of the garlicky mayonnaise. That, inevitably, led to Bob deciding it would be fun if he fed me mouthfuls of bread and fish. I could feel the tension building as I licked his fingers clean of rouille. It wasn't long before Jon and Laura joined in the little game, too, sensing that the "special evening" my husband had talked about was under way.

Instead of the cheese I had intended to finish the meal, Bob surprised me by bringing out a box of handmade chocolates. "I saw them when I was buying the wine," he said. "I know you ladies can't resist something sweet."

Again, the men insisted on feeding us, and by the time we had finished the chocolates and coffee, I was feeling hornier than I had in a long time. All the attention, and the anticipation of what might be about to happen, had me fidgeting in my seat, conscious of how damp my knickers were becoming.

"Why don't we go skinny-dipping?" Laura suggested, looking over to where the surface of the pool rippled in the moonlight.

The others looked eager, but I found myself hanging back. "If you don't mind, I'd rather not. I don't like to go in the water straight after a meal."

"Sarah, sweetheart," Bob said, taking hold of my hand, "that's not the real reason, is it?" I said nothing, and he continued, "Jon had a chat with us the first night we were here, after you went to bed. He told us you're a little sensitive about your scars, but believe me, you don't have to be. Not with us." He stood up, urging me to stand with him. "If you don't want to go to the pool, let's go into the bedroom, and we'll prove it."

I glanced over to Jon, who gave me a reassuring wink. He'd told me no one was going to make me do anything I didn't want to, but I still felt nervous as Bob gently guided me to the bedroom I was sharing with my husband. There were candles on the low bookcase, and Jon busied himself lighting them. The window was partly open, bringing the sweet scent of summer flowers into the room. With Laura's encouragement, I kicked off my sandals and sat down on the bed. She and Bob made themselves comfortable on either side of me, while Jon looked on.

In turn, each of them kissed me: soft, open-mouthed kisses that left me longing for more. The two of them had never worked on me as a team before, but they seemed to know just what to do to make me relax. As Laura nuzzled the nape of my neck while Bob gently teased my nipples through my thin T-shirt, I felt pleasantly limp in their joint embrace. Jon watched avidly, his cock tenting out the front of his shorts, and I wondered how far he would let things go before he became more actively involved.

It was when Bob began to gently tug at the hem of my shirt that I began to panic. I tried to stop him, but he shushed me. "Just trust me. You have nothing to be frightened of."

The next thing I knew, his hand was on my bare skin, circling my stomach. His caress felt so good that I was caught completely off guard when Laura quickly pulled my shirt over my head. It had been far too warm to wear a bra that day, and suddenly I was topless in front of the others, the scars on my breast and flank all too visible. I couldn't remember the last time Jon had seen me like this, never mind anyone else, and I wanted to shrink away and hide so they couldn't look at me.

But instead of making some unwanted comment or averting his gaze, Bob simply kept on stroking me, only now he was touching the part of me I had kept hidden for so long, the part I couldn't bear even my husband seeing.

"Oh, Sarah, so brave and so beautiful..." Laura murmured.

"How can you say that?" I asked. "Look at me; I'm..."

"As fuckable as you always were," Bob told me. "Do you think any of this changes how we feel about you? Are we really that shallow?"

I shook my head. His hand was gradually moving down

over the puckered, scarred skin. His touch was oddly soothing, and when his fingers disappeared under the waistband of my knickers, pushing through my bush to find the soft, wet whorls of my pussy, I lost all resistance. I didn't object when he stripped me of my underwear, even though I was now the only one in the room who was naked. I didn't object when Laura trailed her soft mouth over my skin, kissing smooth and scarred skin alike. And I certainly didn't object when she took one of my nipples in her mouth at the same time as Bob's tongue settled on my clit. Their twin assault was so exciting it almost robbed me of my breath.

I held out a hand, inviting Jon to come closer and join in the action. Greedily, I reached out and unzipped his shorts, letting his hard cock flop into my hand. My fingers circled it, pushing the soft sleeve of skin back and forth along his sturdy length. It was hard to concentrate on wanking him, though, while Bob and Laura continued to lick and suck in tandem. I felt as though my body was one big web of sensation, sparks of pleasure running from my nipples to my clit. It was the closest I had ever come to being worshipped, and I knew it wouldn't take much more of this delicious treatment to give me one of the most spectacular orgasms of my life.

Bob had other ideas, though. He turned me over onto my hands and knees, snuffling his nose into my pussy for a while before announcing that it was time I was fucked. Doggy-style, I remembered from our night in that club in Amsterdam, was his favorite position, only on that occasion it had been Laura he was fucking, squeezing her hanging breasts as he rammed into her from the rear. I turned my head to watch him pull off his shorts and briefs, then roll a condom down over his nicely swollen cock.

Jon took the opportunity to ask, "You're still okay with this?"

I nodded. Bob and Laura had done everything they could to put me at ease. Knowing Jon still found me sexy was one thing, but getting that same affirmation from this experienced couple was starting to make me think I might have been worrying too much. I still wasn't ready to walk along a public beach in a skimpy bikini, but here, with Bob sheathed in ribbed latex and getting into position behind me, I was surprisingly happy to have so much of myself on display.

His cock slid into my juicy depths and his big hands grasped me round the waist, pulling me onto him until his thick length was fully lodged inside me. In front of me, Jon and Laura were beginning to undress each other, my husband freeing her heavy breasts and thumbing her long nipples as she moaned in obvious delight. Bob began to thrust into me with short, stabbing strokes, too excited for anything more than a quickie. That was fine by me; the four of us had all night to fuck, and anyway, his cock was just the right length to hit all the right spots in my over-heated cunt.

The candles flickered in a sudden gust of wind, casting a flattering glow on our sweating, heaving bodies. Bob's hands roamed freely, caressing my breasts, my rib cage and my hips, waking nerve endings in bare skin I'd been so stupid not to let anyone touch since my accident.

He took a firm grip of me as his groin banged against my arse, and I urged him on with the dirtiest language I knew, all my inhibitions long gone. Laura was on her knees now, taking Jon's hard shaft deep into her throat, and that sight, combined with the sudden application of Bob's tricky fingers to my clit, was all it took to bring on a rush of liquid heat, an orgasm so powerful I almost collapsed on the bed.

As Bob's cock spasmed inside me, and Laura continued to give my husband the sucking of his life, I knew the four of us had made a connection that was and always would be much more than skin deep. I cuddled against Bob, resting until both of us were ready to go again and let him trace his hands over the scars I was no longer ashamed to bear.

EDEN

Molly Slate

Try this."

I looked at the offering, then up to his face without pity.

"Darling, that's a fig."

"So?" He thrust it out a little closer, more insistently.

"Well, what exactly am I supposed *to do* with a fig?" I watched him do his sidelong foot-shuffle, that nervous dance I'd seen six times this morning. (He never used to do it.)

"It'll cover those," he muttered, a bare half dart of his eyes toward my upper aberrations. I followed his gaze and stared dumbly.

"Okay, and how exactly am I going to keep it in place, gingersnap? Did you think my nipples had some sort of adhesive properties…?"

His knuckles clenched around the fruit before he let it fly, and the projectile landed hard against my collarbone. He was muttering a string of phrases I'd never heard. I snatched up one of my own and flung it back. My face was making water and I didn't want him to see. We spent the better part of the morning pelting each other with figs. When our bodies were lacquered in sticky purple streams, we stood in the river fifty paces apart and washed with our backs turned.

Noon. My knees were fully scraped and thorns stuck out of my elbows. We'd been crawling over brambles and crags, poking our heads in dark holes, shimmying up trees. Unapproachable places. Unforgiving ground. Like all else, ugly and rife and incomprehensible. He tossed a log at me and told me to carry it in front of my deformities.

"It's heavy."

"Quit complaining."

"Why don't you have to carry a log?"

"Why couldn't you keep your hands to yourself in the orchard?"

"Oh, like you weren't there!"

"You started it."

"Baby."

"*Slut.*"

It slithered off his tongue, thick and salty and full of menace.

"What's that mean?" I whispered.

The lines on him crinkled in confusion. "I don't know," he answered. Turned away. "It's another new one."

It'd been happening since we'd awoken. Unknown words dropping into our heads and off our tongues like apples from the tree. The stranger must've done it. If he was here I could have asked him. But he had left before the sun rose, leaving only a gap between Adam and me, and an unsettling vocabulary making it wider. That's when I learned my face could crack and leak.

Adam had drawn away from me, but I could still feel the word all over my skin.

The muddy log mocked me from the grass. I felt tempted. I was all disaster: blisters, bruises, veins, sagging pouches of skin and unruly hairs. Nothing fit. Covering wasn't enough; I wanted to peel myself off. I tore a sheaf of damp leaves from the nearest branch. My hands stung. *Work, damn it. Just work. Please, let something, let anything work.* I pressed the biggest leaf between my legs and held it there. My free arm folded over my chest, and I chased after Adam, awkward and limping, handicapped with shame.

It shouldn't have been like this.

While I chased Adam, memories chased me. Better days. Yesterdays. A time without question marks or fig-fights or ghastliness or discord. Without time at all. Glory could blend with peace and beauty disappear in tranquility; want and satiation were one. Biting into fruit, soaking under waterfalls, being. Days and moments and infinities lost and lapped in the stride of the sun. Kissing, rolling, unraveling. I couldn't taste any of it. It was trapped behind haze. But I could still taste the stranger in the orchard, could smell his seductions and recall with pain the artful ways he coaxed and taunted our nerves…. *Don't you want to see where the world begins?* We licked promises from his palms.

"What's the matter with you?" I shouted at a peacock. He regarded me steadily. Ignored me, just cockled along, lazy and regal and self-possessed. The animals caught my new scent. I tried to hobble faster. My heart launched itself against my ribs and the word *enemy* landed in my thoughts, leaden.

I had never seen the garden predatory before. The reaching roots and eyes piercing through shadows, all the sticky and barbed poisons. I screamed Adam's name, tripped, face knocked against prickly wet grass. I hurtled forward.

There, over the gulch, I found Adam, rigid with consternation, peering stiffly at the carcass of a deer. I saw him reach out and test the softness of the hide.

Good grief.

"Honey. I think you were better off with the fig."

His neck jerked up. He glared at me with that blinking accusation again, and then something happened—something new. His face cracked. It was waterless, but I stared in amazement before I realized that I had broken open, too, and something new was spilling out, something good and merciful, like balm. Its hands pulled and twisted in my stomach. *This isn't mercy— it's the thing you got in the trade, the thing you're left with when mercy's fled.* It was loud; it was chaos.

Adam was first to come whole again. "Stop laughing at me." *Laughing. He knows its name.* I couldn't stop. It was stomping through me and I had to stand the rampage. I didn't know what my face was breaking into and tried to hide behind my hair.

"Stop it!" He marched to where I stood. I couldn't hold myself up anymore and collapsed against the nearest tree trunk. Still spilling, frantic. He grabbed my hair and wrenched me up.

"What's wrong with you?" There was something unrestrained and frightful in his voice, his grip. "Enough!" He released my hair and shook me by the shoulders. Pulled my face close to his, his voice suddenly low. "You need to be punished."

I fell quiet. That was another new word, but I didn't want to ask what it meant.

He threw me hard against the trunk, snapped a branch from the tree and angrily ripped off its leaves.

"That doesn't work," I protested. "That's not going to cover— "

"Quiet," he growled, seizing my wrist and twisting me around. I was pinned between him and the tree, new deformities exposed.

"Adam…"

"Hold still."

The air whistled behind me, and a flash later something live and angry sliced my skin.

"What are you doing?" I gasped.

Another whistle, another flicker of pain. *Agony.* It slipped into my mind but stayed unspoken.

"Teaching you." His voice was soft, vicious, strange. I writhed away but he pushed me back, commanding me with threat in his throat to stay where I was. The branch whipped down again, stinging me in places that had never known pain. Words fell with the strokes—*searing, misery, vengeance, cruel*—until the fire obliterated language and thought. I almost bit the bark. The rod lashed across my backside, shoulders, thighs. Sounds leapt out of me, I ground my teeth, water twisted down my face. *Of course, if you agree, you may be punished….* So the stranger in the orchard had told us, only then I hadn't understood. I wept bitterly against the tree as the pain mounted and reached its crest. *Wept.* I understood now.

I don't know how I stayed there, except that I suddenly feared the man who held it more than I feared the stick itself.

I was too absorbed in self-pity to notice, at first, when he flung the switch aside. My arms grasped the tree for support as I heaved against it. Something else was happening, somewhere deep, something besides pain. I didn't want to look at it. Then came Adam's hands, unexpectedly gentle on my shoulders, peeling me from the bark and pulling me close. He held me while I sobbed.

"Why?" I choked when words could come again.

Only silence, thick with thought. He stroked my face, tenderly. "Things are different now."

I shoved him off.

"That's all? That's all you can say?" I screamed. I staggered back, unthinking. I stared at him in horror. Leaves had fallen, nothing was hidden. Our deformities glared beneath the light, alien and unkind.

"I don't know what you are," I cried. "We used to be—we were part of each other. But those...it's not right." Everything on him sickened me, everything on me confounded. I felt laughter and punishment, madness and horror. And then, more brutal than any of the other arrivals, came the latest sudden word, *alone.* "You're different. I'm not...I don't know how any of these parts fit. All I know is that you are what you are and I'm something else, and it will always be like that, and I'll never be able to get inside."

I fell to my knees. I wanted to cry again, but I was empty.

Nearing twilight. We worked in silence, backs to each other, painstakingly weaving flowers and pasting leaves to each other with the sticky innards of figs. Dressing.

I was wandering through a maze, running against all the sudden walls between things. Dividing different actions, feelings, Adam and me. In the other days, nothing had been so distinct, so immutable, oblique. To eat, to sing, to reach for each other—it all bled together, all came from and led to the same source. You didn't have to hoist yourself over a bulwark to go from you to him, tired to wakeful, hungry to content. We didn't have hierarchies or judgments or curiosities or fears. We weren't deformed.

And snaking through these thoughts were memories of the orchard, shivering visions, bright recollections of how it felt to be whipped against the tree. Things would come alive, things that still hadn't been assigned names.

I made a flimsy girdle of dandelions that would cover the

worst of it, snuck a glance at Adam—he was having a difficult time. Kept trying to address his problem with different experiments and grunting in discomfort, sudden pain. It was sensitive. He hadn't figured out how to handle it.

"Do you need help?"

That got him all defensive. "You've helped enough," he spat.

Honestly. I'd be hearing that one 'til the end of time. "Listen, sparky, I know you're upset and all, but there were three of us in that orchard."

"I don't want to discuss it."

"God, you are *so* full of hang-ups."

"Shut it, spare rib."

I turned away and muttered curses against his problem. Let locusts eat it, let it break out in sores. I examined my garment of weeds and felt superior. He stewed and brooded, huffily, until: "What are 'hang-ups'?"

I didn't answer. Didn't know how. We went back to work in silence. When the visions came, my eyes closed and my hands moved, my heart sore in my chest and my skin taut. I wanted to reach, to pull, but I met a wall.

Adam never used to give me trouble. We didn't call each other names or throw things. He was a dear little dumpling. A sweet smiling sugarplum. He'd say, *Eve, I brought you a butterfly.* Or *Eve, come see the color of the moon tonight.* As if it was his birthright to give me wonders. It was adorable. He would absolutely never say, *Damn it, Eve, quit following me around, I can't handle clingy right now.* He wouldn't say, *I just need space.*

Fine. Let him have it. I'd give him all the me-free space he pleased.

"You want space? You can have fucking Siberia!"

* * *

An uneasy dusk finally came. We'd wandered away, looking for help, being apart. *This is stupid,* I thought. *This is dumb and stupid.* I looked at the sparrows and toadstools and squirrels and canaries and possums and the thick black lines drawn between all of us, choking us, and started throwing rocks. *And I hate him.* What wasn't to hate about him? Hideous, wicked, frustrating anatomy. Sinewed hands. Strained muscles in his neck. That audacious, impertinent problem of his, causing disasters. I learned it wasn't only my eyes that made water. *He makes me cry everywhere.*

"I hate your stupid nose!" I threw a stone against a cliffside. "And your stupid knees. And your eyebrows! And your overly large knuckles! And your stupid hair!"

I threw and screamed. It was like running full throttle toward all Adam's walls and smashing against them. As I ran, his terrible parts materialized and crashed, sometimes magnified, minimized, blurred, colored—a wrist, an iris, a fretful finger—pulling together like a night sky that starts with a single impatient star. And as I raced, things began to show differently; they weren't walls anymore, but doors, secret chambers I had the key to, could open and find his dark tendrils, his infant laugh, his scowl, his gangly arms, his certain hands, his blistered feet.

I was leaning against a willow trunk, eyes closed, when I heard his step. My eyes opened and I trembled.

He stood ten feet away, just staring. I'd never seen that look before. At least, I hadn't noticed.

His eyes traced the whole length of my body, starting with my wounded feet, along my calves, fig-stained thighs, the stems and petals hanging low across my hips. They rested long on the leaves over the most garish deformities. He looked hypnotized.

"Look at you," he murmured.

"Don't," I protested, face flushing ruthlessly.

His eyes held intent and purpose that he had never shown before. He came nearer; a part of me strained for his touch, another part wanted to wither and hide.

"Just look at you." And he did, as though I were a gift for him to unwrap.

I stared sideways at the grass and squirmed, a perfect mirror of his morning shiftiness. He gently turned my face to him. I couldn't plead. His hands traveled lingeringly to my waist and he tore a leaf from my breast with his teeth.

I gave the tiniest gasp. He locked eyes with me. I saw steel and certainty. He bit another leaf.

"Adam..."

Instead of ordering me to be silent, he stopped my questions with a long and sudden kiss. New words were pouring. *Urgency, frenzy, passion.*

"Passion," I breathed when Adam surfaced.

"What?"

I grabbed his hair. Nails drove hungry into his scalp. "Give me new words," I begged.

He flicked off another leaf and teased me subtly with his tongue. "Please!"

But Adam was in no hurry. His deft tongue busied itself with the newly wakened liveliness at my breasts before he saw fit to appease me. "Mystery," he whispered. Acutely, as though it were the first time we'd touched, I felt his caresses, his grip on my back, his mouth on my ear. I felt the word breathe on my neck. "Need."

"More," I whispered.

Adam's hands clasped with confidence, owning all deformities, aberrations, wrongs. But his breaths were shredded. "Dreams. Choices. Danger. Art."

Don't you want to see where the world begins...? Animals and storms and mighty crashes of water swelled inside me. It was clamor and chaos. I shook. I was sweating, secreting, pouring onto the earth, onto him. I wanted to hold him, keep him, throttle and destroy and crumple and melt. I clasped his neck and kissed him with an angry gratitude. I reached to the problem he couldn't handle, trusting myself.

"Metaphor," he muttered, as I wrought what I could. "Nuance. Rage." He was coming toward wordlessness. I was close to letting something free, but he grabbed my wrists and pinned my arms over my head. "Submission," he snarled. The sound made me pant. "Will."

The slow waltzing lilt of his mouth at my leaves gave way to ravenous gorging until I was left undone. Disguises stripped. I could feel his triumph, and I couldn't stop shaking from the new miracle of him, the joy of opening, climbing. "Discovery," he said. It was wicked, and wrong, and we knew that now.

Adam's voice came faster, rougher. Insistent fingers reached and the walls collapsed. "Torment. Power. Freedom. Shame." I bit my lip and thought I tasted blood. "Exile. Knowledge. Love."

Then some power ripped through me, exploded the walls, felled the towers, rattled my bones. I rent the leaves sticking to Adam, not with any of his studied sophistication, but desperately. He let my arms go and I flung them round his neck and my legs around his back. The bark was tearing at me. I wanted the worst, I wanted the unspeakable, the abhorrent, the unblessed, the wound. And he would yield it, would indulge, would join with me as strangers and aliens do—not falling into something but creating, wreaking havoc on the ground, on each other. It was close. It was almost—

Adam stopped. Pulled back, stared in my eyes, hard. And I

looked at him, this whole new person, this new world.

"Transgression," he whispered, and then threw into me. *"Sin."*

We flung ourselves into our catastrophe, knees shaking against the willow, until we found the softness of the grass and tumbled through it battle ready, willing and loving and uninnocent and shorn; until we rolled, together, naked, out of Eden.

THREE STOPS AWAY

Heidi Champa

As I walked down the steps to the subway, my fingers were tingling, and it wasn't just because of the temperature. It was cold, but my shaking body had less to do with my forgotten scarf and more to do with what lay ahead of me that morning. When I reached the platform, I looked around at my fellow commuters, wondering who was going to be brave enough to join me. They looked unassuming enough, reading papers or books, bobbing their heads to the music pumping directly into their heads. The crowd wasn't as big as I'd expected, but there were more than enough people to make me sweat in my winter coat. I'd spent hours picking out my clothes, making sure I looked good for what was about to happen.

The train was coming; the telltale whoosh of air hit me square in the face as the screeching and scraping grew louder and louder. The crowd around me jostled forward, and I was swept up in the momentum as the doors opened and we all piled inside. Following the flow, I grabbed the first seat I could find and found myself breathing heavily as the doors dinged and shuddered to a close. As if on cue, everyone around me started shucking off his or her pants and skirts, pulling them off and shoving them into bags. I hesitated, watching all the commuters joining in the fun, but I stayed frozen in my seat. I wanted to join in, that was the whole reason I'd gotten on the train. But something was holding me back. The train started moving, but my pants were still right where they should be.

My cheeks flushed in some sort of bizarre reverse embarrassment. Wearing pants actually made me stick out like a sore thumb, with most of the other riders proudly displaying their panties, boxers and briefs. I thought of the time I had spent searching for the panties I was wearing, trying to find the most flattering fit and style. My bedroom floor was littered with inappropriate candidates, each one discarded for various offenses. All that work had been for nothing, I realized as I sat on the molded plastic seat, everyone else showing off his or her wild, crazy or vintage undergarments. One pair in particular caught my attention. The purple-and-yellow-patterned boxers made me notice the nicely shaped legs they sat on, the dark hair accenting the pale skin perfectly. My eyes continued upward, taking in the tall frame of the rider, who was also looking at me. His eyes immediately dropped to my denim-covered legs and he smiled broadly. My mouth fell open as I watched him walk toward me, his bag slipping off his shoulder. His naked legs had me mesmerized, but I managed to meet his eyes when he stopped in front of me.

"Don't you think you're a little overdressed for this ride?"

His eyes again raked my legs, my clothing all the more obvious among all the other naked legs.

"I guess I chickened out."

My face burned as he sat down next to me, a presumptuous

hand resting on my knee. I knew I should knock it away or at the very least question him about it. But I did neither, choosing instead to revel in the heat of his palm and the smell of his cologne.

"Chickened out? Come on, there's still time. It's not like you're alone. It's kind of the whole point of being on the train today. Just yank 'em off. I promise, it's painless. Well, it's cold, but other than that, you should be fine. After all, you *are* breaking the rules. That's why they call it the No Pants Subway Ride."

I knew he was right, but something was still holding me back from joining the crowd. As I was about to voice my objections, he grabbed my hand and pulled me up, our bodies almost touching. I grasped the metal pole in the center of the car, steadying myself against the sway of the train. I focused on staying upright and tried to buy time to keep my pants on. When his hand dropped to my belt buckle, I reached to stop him, but instead I found my fingers twined with his. He leaned his face right in front of mine and killed me with his whisper.

"Come on, you know you want to."

His eyes were such a deep brown, I felt like he was staring right into me. My objections started to melt, becoming less and less important as he pressed harder against me. Letting go of his hand, I didn't prevent him from opening my belt and buttons, and my pants were soon pooled around my ankles. I stood stunned, the rest of the passengers oblivious, as he bent down and pulled my pants from my feet. I waited for him to stand up right away, but when I looked at him, I noticed his head moving toward my thigh. I darted my eyes around the car, expecting to see everyone staring at us. But no one seemed to notice as he licked and kissed his way toward my now-exposed panties. His hand pressed into my flesh, the pad of his thumb stroking circles near the back of my knee.

Before anyone could become suspicious, he stood again, handing me my pants. His lips covered mine with the same gentle touch as he had used on my leg, his tongue exploring my mouth insistently. We pulled apart, both panting a little.

"See. That wasn't so bad, was it?"

"I guess not."

"Nice panties, by the way."

The time I had taken picking out the perfect pair had obviously paid off. The black silk with the ruffled bottom were my favorite naughty pair of panties, and I could think of no better place to show them off than on a subway car. He put his arm around my back as if we had known each other for years. To anyone who might look our way, we were just another couple having a good time on No Pants Subway Ride day. But the fact was, he was a stranger slipping his finger into the waistband of my panties. He turned and faced me, our bodies close, hiding the fact that the tip of his finger had made its way to my moist slit. He stared down into my eyes, his lips parting as he touched my clit. My teeth sank into my lip to hold back the moan, my tight nub responding to his touch. We shifted together as the car came to a halt, more people pressing inside to take part in the bottomless journey.

I grabbed his wrist, encouraging him to go farther, and his finger entered my wet cunt with one easy motion. My grip on the metal pole was slipping, my palms and back clammy with sweat. Our legs rubbed together, his soft hair tickling me and raising goose bumps on my skin. He held me closer: one finger, now two, moved slowly and deeply inside me. I broke away from his gaze to again check and see if anyone was onto our game. If any of the other riders had noticed, they didn't let on. The only thing different about this train ride was the abundance of naked legs, not what we were secretly doing in the center of the car. He brought me back to him with a kiss, and I could feel his erection against my hip. I reached down and pressed his dick with my palm, careful not to let the head pop out of the trap door in his boxers.

With each stop, more and more people filled the car, removing their pants before adding to the cacophony of noise with their own laughter. I ignored them all, focused only on the man in front of me as the shimmying car and his insistent fingers brought me closer and closer to orgasm. His thumb had joined the fun, rubbing over my clit with subtle pressure. Before I could gasp or moan he kissed me again, swallowing any sound that would have drawn more attention to us. As the moving party went on all around us, I relished the feel of his forehead resting against mine, the firm feel of his hand on the small of my back. Grasping at his jacket, I tried to remain calm, but the growing pressure in my cunt was making it very difficult to stay cool. His knee slipped between my thighs, and I clamped down on it tightly.

The car came to a halt one last time, and he froze, holding me hostage on the edge until the car started moving again. His fingers pushed inside me even deeper, and the gentle pressure on my clit turned into an unrelenting strum. I was desperate to throw my head back and scream my joy out into the metal car, but I didn't. Coming in silence has never been my strong suit, but when my eyes closed and I felt myself tumble, all I could focus on were the intense waves of pleasure crashing over me. I dug my face into him, pressing my mouth into his sweater-clad chest to keep myself quiet. My pussy tightened around his fingers, the in-and-out movement replaced with a swirling wiggle. He held me tight, substituting his strength for my own, until my legs relaxed and could support me again.

We pulled apart a bit, and things slowly returned to normal, his eyes back on mine. There were no words to explain what just happened, nothing to say to the handsome stranger who had made me come in the middle of a crowded subway car. His smile broke the tension and his kiss made me smile back. The train jerked and stopped, both of us leaning into each other to ride out the force.

"This is my stop."

"Me, too."

We stepped onto the platform, putting our pants back on before heading back into the harsh cold. I looked at him, not knowing what to do next. Luckily for me, he took control of the situation, just as he had on the train. He pressed a business card into my hand and kissed me one last time.

"Those really are great panties."

THE SUSHI GIRL

Anika Gupta

T he light felt hot on my bare stomach. I shifted and then tensed
my abs when a piece of sashimi drifted dangerously close to
my ribs. Goddamn, it was going to be a long night. I couldn't
get up. Tiny leaves covered in tuna rolls pinned my chest and
hips to the table. Artsy mounds of sashimi sat atop the small
mountains of my breasts. I kept my arms behind my head and
my legs together.

If it weren't for the air-conditioning, I would have started to
sweat. It would have been unseemly. Finally, nearly thirty minutes
late, they came in: a group of men in blue and black suits. They
were laughing, but when they saw me they fell momentarily
silent. They put their jackets over the backs of their seats and
sat down, one each at my elbows and knees, one at my head and
one at my feet. A party of six is the ideal number.

The waiter hovered in the background. His name was
Fernando. His family had moved to the States from the Domin-
ican Republic years ago. His aunts and uncles back home

thought he was a doctor and would call him for medical advice. He would give them bogus antidotes so they wouldn't realize that he was actually in food prep.

Fernando never had the temerity to touch me, which was good. I would have knocked his balls off.

This was the first party of the evening and Fernando came forward to ask, in his nasal voice, if they knew the procedure.

"How hard can it be?" quipped one, a blond man with large hands and a square face. I didn't like him. In a few months he, like all the other men at the table, would lose his house in a bet on dubious mortgage-backed securities. The fund they were here to celebrate would be one of Wall Street's most spectacular failures, a cautionary tale about greed. But at the moment, he was just another rich diner.

One of them raised his chopsticks and clicked them, the sound loud in the quiet room.

"What are the rules?" he asked. His face and his fondness for rules reminded me of a boyfriend I'd had once, a Jewish boy from Minnesota. This man wasn't looking at me.

This question I hadn't expected, but Fernando had. He reeled them off with the ease of a movie actor taking a scene for the tenth time in a row.

"...And no touching with bare hands," he finished.

Underneath the light, I squirmed. I felt a trail of sweat starting in one of my armpits and felt gross. I wondered if they'd notice.

The Jew was the first to move. To his right there was an Indian guy, glasses on, clearly shocked at the banquet of flesh in front of him. The blond took it all in stride. He gazed at me with calm boredom, as if he could be anywhere. Their companions, more successful than they, had all been here before.

With the end of his chopstick, the Jew tapped one of the

pieces of tuna roll set innocently beside my navel. I felt it slide down my side and land on the table. He speared it with his chopstick, dipped it in the sesame oil provided, and put it in his mouth.

"I feel like we should be drunk," said the blond, "in order to do this."

I felt like I should be drunk. The Indian was next. His hand rose, and he circled it over my ankle. I wanted to get up and look at him, but I couldn't. I felt the sudden release of pressure as he lifted a piece of sushi. My knee felt bare; I shivered. He tossed the sushi into his mouth without dipping.

The blond was next. He reached forward. I felt the slow wet slide of a leaf along my ribs. He didn't wait to finish but grabbed the sushi, the tines of chopsticks denting my side, creating pricks of sensation. My blood rushed toward him. He bungled the sushi halfway to his mouth and had to fumble for it in his lap. His colleagues laughed.

They ordered a round of sake and got friendlier. The sashimi was untouched, but my knees were bare, my naked legs laid out like an offering. The light pooled hotly over my ankles, but my stomach was cool. The twin spots on my breasts where the sashimi rested were cold.

I felt the weight of the sushi on my abdomen disappear. The leaves had slid out of place, a few of them gathered between my thighs. I pinched my legs more tightly together.

The blond broached the sashimi first. I felt the rounded end of his right chopstick glance off the side of my breast. He coughed and reached forward. He pinched the sashimi tightly, raised it in an arc to his face. I saw the white rice disappear into his mouth, watched his throat bump up and down as he swallowed. He looked down again, contemplating the sashimi, eyes grazing my bare breast without judgment. He smiled to himself, sat down.

At the far end of the room, I heard the door swing open. Fernando went to it. He whispered. Another round of sake had come, and the men were drinking it, laughing about people they knew from the office. One of the men, the one at my right elbow, had developed a pink flush. They had forgotten I was there, and I floated on a cloud of heat and distance, connecting to them only when their slippery chopsticks accidentally grazed my arms, thighs, ribs. We were strangers in the same place; even though they were seeing me naked, it wasn't me they were seeing.

"There's a call from a Mr. Hatsumomo," said Fernando. The room went silent. The blond man leaned back in his chair. I could see him frown out of the corner of my eye.

"Now?" he said. Fernando's look must have been convincing, because he got up and went to take the call. A minute later he reappeared, looking grave. "Rick, Neel, come here." The Indian and yet another went away. Three of the places at the banquet were empty. A tense silence had fallen over us all, and suddenly I was uncomfortable, aware of being naked, cramped. Blood had collected in the small of my back; my shoulders ached.

The last three waited without talking to each other.

"I'm going to use the men's," said one of them at last—the Jewish one. He got up and stepped out.

"That means he's gone to check his BlackBerry," said the blond to his companion, a dark-haired man with an eyebrow ridge like a cliff. "He'll be gone for a few hours."

The companion laughed, but it wasn't the friendly laughter of a friend. Then he, too, got up.

"Stretch my legs," he said. The room was empty. I tried, imperceptibly, to shift. I was suddenly aware of the blond man in the room, the drape of his blue shirt as he put his arm across the back of the now-empty chair next to him. When he took a sip of his drink, I could hear him swallow. He looked at his watch. I watched him without his realizing it.

At last, he looked up at me. He seemed to notice the dinner again. Idly, he picked up the chopsticks, turning them around in his hand as if he'd never seen them before. With the same lethargy, he reached out and dragged one rounded end along my right rib, circling my breast. I breathed in deeply as the leaf over my right nipple shivered. The sashimi listed to the side. He tapped at it but didn't pick it up. I looked at his face, but his gaze was fixed on his hands.

Again, he traced the curving slope, and finally the leaf slid, a slow cool slide down into the shadow between my breasts. He got up and leaned over me. His figure was vast, and so was his shadow. He tapped the tine against the ridge of my exposed nipple, almost by accident. I looked at him sharply but his eyes were on the sushi, cradled against my body.

I waited for him to retrieve it. He squeezed the edge of the leaf between the chopsticks, and I felt the leaf slide coolly, leaving a dry trail down the muscular plane between my ribs, the soft rise of the fat between. I pulled in my stomach and the soft lump passed over my navel. I bit my lip when it reached the juncture of my legs, coming to rest at last in the place where, in more ancient times, a fig leaf would have belonged. It sat, heavy, right over my clitoris. When he tapped the sashimi again with his chopsticks, the pressure went through the soft rice and through my skin. I squeezed my legs together so tightly that the muscles in my thighs were shaking.

I tried not to say anything. He tapped the sushi again. This time, almost infinitesimally, I let my thighs relax. The cool roll tumbled down between my thighs, brushing against the soft lips of my lower body, and it landed on the table right between.

I watched his back as he dipped his chopsticks in sesame oil.

They rose, glistening with the oil. Then, with infinite care, he followed the trail of the sushi, leaving a slick line like a snake's wake down my body. I fought the urge to move my hips as the chopsticks glazed their downward path between those same soft lips. He did not press. I gasped as my lips were spread apart, as he spread his chopsticks to grab the piece of sushi. When he pulled it up, the rice passed through my pussy lips, over the entrance to my vagina—a soft scrape. I felt a few grains of rice come away.

His face was still in shadow as he brought the sushi to his lips and slowly ate it. His lips were very pink in the light; the sushi looked gray. He took another drink of sake. I kept my arms tight behind my head. My nipples were hard and I willed them to soften.

With one hand he picked up the dish of oil. I watched his arm pass over me, saw the gold spill of oil, narrow, spilling toward the shaded crevice. And then I felt the touch of it, the beads of oil unexpectedly hard between the swooping bones of my hips. It was warm. It dripped slowly down to the space between my legs, rolling down my skin like sweat. I couldn't help my breathing.

The smooth rounded end of one chopstick found its way between my wet lips. He swirled the tip around a clinging grain of rice. I pulled myself back against the hot warmth of the table, back into the light, as the chopsticks probed. When he slid the chopsticks and the single grain of rice away, my body nearly went with them. He ate the grain of rice.

I waited as he chewed. A few more minutes passed. He reached for another grain of rice. This time the pressure was almost unbearable. I pushed my nails into the back of my head, filling my lungs with air, to resist the slow slide of the chopsticks down to another one of the scattered grains. This one he pinched tightly, pulled up slowly. The soft grain rubbed against my sensitive skin, the air rushed against my open legs, cooling me, chilling me.

For a few seconds he looked at the grain of rice. Then he put it into his mouth. I was shaking. A fine mist of sweat had come up over my body. I was afraid he could tell.

When he went for the third grain, I caught my tongue between my teeth and pinched it until the cells complained. This time, as he pulled the grain up, he pushed hard against me. I heard someone breathing deeply and realized it was me. I pushed my legs farther apart, almost a plea. I ground my muscles into the table as the smooth filed tips of the chopsticks searched for the lost rice. My ribs came inward, my entire body like a river falling down over a cliff, all my blood rushing in one direction.

He pushed farther, lightly, and I rasped. At last his chopsticks came slightly apart, then together. He fished the grain of rice out, chewed it meditatively. I willed him to look at me, but I was afraid of it, too. He gripped his chopsticks again. If he touched me another time I would lose hold of the ocean. At that moment, the door swung open, sending cool air into the room. I sagged, sorry, disappointed, as he turned his face to the door. It was the Indian. He rushed up to us, his eyes only for his colleague, his face wild. He didn't notice the tension in my limbs; it was as if I'd disappeared.

"Get out here, man. Rick's really worried about some-thing."

"Okay." He nodded. I watched as he put the chopsticks down. I exhaled loudly enough for him to hear it, but still the dark wing of his eyelid didn't waver. He turned away from the table, from me. I saw his back, his legs, the nape of his neck, in a way I hadn't noticed before. The back of his shirt had a small wet spot in it. He walked out.

He didn't come back. The room returned to normalcy, the air settled, the golden haze over me grew dim. I reached a single, desperate, careful hand down between my legs. The smell of fish and seaweed filled my nostrils. My body was slippery with sesame oil. I circled one finger down, down, until I found the last lost grain of rice. When I pulled my find away, I came.

I lay looking at the light until the pinpricks in my body stopped. My sweat cooled. My breathing returned to normal.

The men didn't come back, even though I waited for half an hour. After that, Fernando came in, looking worried. He said the men had left in a rush, without finishing their meal.

That night marked the start of the national unraveling. I stayed at the job for another three months, but financial losses eventually forced the restaurant to close. A few weeks later I would see those same six men in a picture in the newspaper, next to an article announcing that their fund had collapsed, unable to cover its debts.

As far as I know, I never met any of them again. Once, walking past Central Park, I saw a man I thought was Neel sitting with a coffee, staring at the bare trees. But he didn't recognize me.

THIS NIGHT

Suzanne V. Slate

This night is yours.

I am late getting home from work and I know this means trouble. Out of breath, I rush into the apartment and see you already sitting in your leather club chair, arms resting on the padded armrests, drumming your fingers impatiently. As you glare at me, I stammer out an apology about a delay on the subway, but you immediately order me silent. You are still dressed from work in your favorite old-school gray suit, tie, dress shirt and immaculately clean wingtip shoes.

You order me to strip. You stare at me unblinkingly as I remove my clothes, and I am suddenly self-conscious. Usually we undress together, and I am surprised at how shy I feel. I wish I'd had time today to get a wax and a pedicure. I hope I pass your scrutiny.

Naked, I kneel at your feet. Obeying your orders, I place my hands behind my neck and straighten my back, pulling my belly in and thrusting my breasts forward. I wait as you examine me, nervous under your stern gaze, scarcely breathing. I do not dare to look at you. You nudge my thighs farther apart with the toe of your shoe, and I bow my head to acknowledge the correction. Despite my vulnerability, or perhaps because of it, I feel my pussy lips start to pulsate and swell.

You begin to play.

Still sitting in the club chair, you trace around and under my breasts with the tip of your shoe. The cold hard leather feels harsh and impersonal, yet the touch stiffens my nipples instantly. I suppress a shudder, mindful of your instructions to keep still. Your foot trails down my belly and between my legs, and you begin stroking my inner cunt lips with the tip of your wingtips. I have to fight the instinct to draw my legs together and push away your shoe, which is now probing the entrance to my cunt casually and clinically. But I do not move. Slowly you withdraw your shoe, and I see it is already glistening wet. For some reason I feel ashamed. You toss a handkerchief to me, and I hastily wipe the leather dry. You lean back in your club chair and grin, taking pleasure in my discomfort.

After I have finished, you take the handkerchief from me and put it back in your suit pocket. Your cock strains against the fabric of your suit pants. I stare at it, and you watch me stare. Slowly, you unfasten your belt buckle and slide the belt out of your pant loops, one by one. My breath catches in my throat. Gathering the smooth black leather strap into one hand, you order me to lie across your lap.

I crawl forward on my hands and knees, apprehensive. You've never used a belt before. I stretch across your lap and wait, eyes squeezed shut, trying so hard to be good. You raise one hand and I cringe, waiting for the blow. But rather than whipping me, you drop the belt and begin to stroke my bare back, complimenting me on my obedience. This was only a test.

I am grateful. As your hands travel freely over my body I start to relax, enjoying being petted and admired. I can't help it: I tip my ass up to meet your hand, silently urging you to stroke my clit and enter me with your fingers. My hips flex and twist, and I rub my nipples against the smooth fabric of your suit pants. A soft moan of frustration escapes my lips before I can clamp them shut.

That was a mistake. You are not in the mood to cater to me. Roughly, you push me upright and order me to unfasten your pants. I obey hastily, relishing the sight of your cock unfurling and springing free of the fabric. I want to grab it and take it into my mouth, but I know better. I wait.

We both sit, frozen, you watching me while I watch your cock. Finally, you can't stand it anymore. You grab my hair and push my head into your lap. I fall upon your cock, taking the head into my mouth while I grab your shaft firmly and start stroking. Precome quickly coats my lips and chin. Your cock becomes streaked with my red lipstick as I move up and down, up and down, as you press my head into your lap, over and over again.

Soon you relax your grip on my head and arch your head backward. You are in your own world now, on the verge of coming, and at this moment I exist only to service you. I intensify my movements, rocking and sucking, and you thrust your hips off the chair to meet my mouth. The whole world centers around your cock. At the last second, you grab my hair and jerk my head backward, staring right into my eyes as you come in my face. You spray my cheeks, lips and open mouth. I gasp for breath, feeling your hot come drip out my mouth, down my chin and onto your suit pants. I cast my eyes down and see red lipstick smeared everywhere.

After you release your grip, I sit back on my heels with my

thighs open wide. I am drenched. Again you toss me your hand-kerchief. Gently, I wipe your cock and then my face, as you stare at me, grinning.

Suddenly the doorbell rings. It's the pizza guy. My orgasm will have to wait.

You order me to crawl on my hands and knees to the door, slapping my ass hard to hurry me along. I comply, but as I approach the door there is a new knot in the pit of my stomach. So far our games have only involved each other. Surely you wouldn't dare introduce another person into the mix.

I am wrong. You tell me to stand and answer the door, and by the tone of your voice I can tell you mean business. Before I can stop myself I open my mouth to protest, but all that comes out is a weak whimper. Your gaze darkens and I avert my eyes. Standing behind the door, I slowly open it and the pizza guy enters the room. He stands in the middle of the room, facing you. "Close the door," you say sharply. The guy turns around just as I am closing the door, leaving myself exposed and uncov-ered. My arms twitch, moving almost involuntarily to cover my breasts and crotch, but I know better than that. I press them to my sides. I stand naked before both of you, head bowed, feeling vulnerable as never before.

The pizza guy doesn't know which way to turn. He looks nervously from me to you and back again. Mostly he stares at the floor. But eventually he figures out that he won't get in any trouble for looking. So he does what he wants: taking his cue from you, he stares boldly at me, looking me up and down, eyes lingering on my breasts and pussy. I stand stock still, barely breathing.

After what seems like forever, you break the spell. "Take the pizza to the kitchen," you say. "I'll get the money." The guy hands me the pizza and I head to the kitchen. It's only fifteen or twenty feet, but with both sets of eyes burning into me it feels like the longest walk of my life. I want to run as fast as I can, but at the same time I am conscious of every bounce and undulation of my breasts and buttocks as I step, so I walk as smoothly as I can on my trembling legs. Finally, I make it to the kitchen. I lean over the sink, struggling to catch my breath, listening for the front door to close behind the pizza guy so I can safely emerge again.

You are not going to make it that easy. You call me back out, and so I have to obey. I walk back into the living room with the same hypercautious gait. Both of you stare at my breasts as they bob up and down. "Come here and give him the money," you direct me. You pull some money out of your wallet, but you don't hold it out for me—you hold it low and close to you so I have to bend over to retrieve it, giving the pizza guy a good look at my ass and pussy lips from behind. I can't believe this is happening; it feels like I am in a dream. I'm almost faint with humiliation but deep down somewhere I am also aroused by my own powerlessness. I stumble as I straighten up and you reach for my forearm, steadying me, studying my face carefully to see how much I can take.

I can take it. I cross the room and hand the pizza guy the money, keeping as much distance between us as I dare. For a moment I fear he is going to grab one of my breasts but he doesn't. Our eyes meet for a second and he smiles at me. I wonder if he can smell your come on my face. You call out from your seat in the club chair, reminding me to give him a good tip. "It's okay, sir," the guy stammers as he follows me to the door. "You already gave me one."

After he leaves I close the door behind him, sinking against it. I am exhausted, completely drained. When at last I raise my eyes to look at you, you are smiling at me. "Hungry?" you ask.

The clock chimes the hour and the game is over. You jump out of your chair, wrap me in a robe, put your arm around my shoulder and lead me to the kitchen.

This night is mine.

I take my time getting home from work, stopping to get a wax and pedicure before boarding the subway. At home you are anxiously waiting for me, sitting in your club chair with your arms immobile on the padded armrests. You are clad in my favorite old-school gray suit, tie, white dress shirt and spotlessly clean wingtips, just as I had ordered. When I enter you lower your eyes. I look you up and down. You pass my scrutiny.

I stand over you and order you to watch me strip. You shyly raise your eyes and look as, one by one, my clothes fall to the floor, very slowly, until at last I am standing naked before you. You watch as I gracefully kneel on the floor. I sit back on my heels with my back arched, breasts thrust forward, thighs opened wide. I stare at you, proudly on display, daring you to look at me, to touch me. Enjoying the rush of power I feel from being on display like this, I feel my pussy lips start to pulsate and swell.

I begin to play.

I kneel on the floor with my knees apart and sit for a moment, letting you watch me. I stare long and hard at your cock, which is straining against the confines of your suit pants. You glance down at yourself and cast a quick pleading look at me before averting your eyes again. To your great surprise, I do as you want: I slowly unzip your pants, drawing your smooth, hot cock out, stroking and squeezing it from root to tip. As soon as it is free of your clothing it springs in the air and I slap it gently, watching it bounce near my parted lips. I flick the sparkling drop of precome with my tongue.

Your questioning eyes follow every move I make. I bend

forward over your cock, cradling my breasts with my hands, pressing them together on either side of your shaft, and I begin to move slowly up and down. My ass moves back and forth and I exaggerate each movement, enjoying the effect my body has on you. My red lips tease the tip of your cock with each thrust, wetting it as I lap up your precome. You are trying so hard to be good, struggling with all your might to keep your arms glued to the chair and your hips still as you watch my breasts gliding up and down your cock.

Suddenly I draw back and rise to my feet, slapping your cock hard. A sharp moan of protest escapes your lips before you quickly clamp them shut.

That was a mistake. I am not in the mood to cater to you. I straddle one of the arms of the club chair and rest my bare pussy on the back of your hand. I can feel your forearms tense as I glide back and forth over your bare skin, at first gently and then with more force. Soon your hand and the French cuff of your shirt are damp with my juices. The stiff cuff connects with my clit and suddenly I cannot bear any more teasing, either. I reach down and turn your hand so your palm is facing up. I sit on your hand so it cradles my pussy and resume my rocking, pressing my clit hard on the heel of your hand as your fingers graze the opening of my cunt.

You moan in frustration. Instinctively your fingers twitch, seeking entry, and your hips flex and twist in the deep cushions of the club chair. Although I am barely able to stop anymore, I force myself to draw up and glare at you in silent reprimand. Immediately, I feel your fingers relax. You stop moving and bow your head to acknowledge the correction.

I take your relaxed index finger and guide it into my cunt. Your other fingers, gently curled, graze my inner and outer lips, my inner thighs, my asshole. I resume riding hard against the heel of your hand. My clit has stiffened into a hard little pearl that grates against your palm. This time you obey the rules and keep still as you watch my body tense. My head arches back. I am in my own world now, on the verge of coming, and at this moment you exist only to service me. I thrust my breasts in your face and writhe on your open palm. The whole world centers around my cunt. I coil tighter and tighter, every muscle inside and out contracting impossibly taut, until at last I explode, screaming as every muscle and nerve in my body releases and lets go. I rock back and forth on your hand, gradually slowing my thrusts as my breathing returns to normal.

At last I open my eyes. I lean back and look at you. We are drenched with sweat and my juices. I order you to zip up and wipe us clean with your handkerchief. Gently you wipe my cunt and then your hand, as I stare at you, grinning.

Suddenly the doorbell rings. It's the pizza guy. Your orgasm will have to wait.

I speak sharply to you: "Stay there," I say. "I'll get the door." Your eyes widen in protest but I merely smile in response. I know what you're thinking: except for once before, our games have only involved each other, and that one time, I was miserable. Surely I wouldn't dare introduce another person into the mix again.

You are wrong. I direct you to place your arms back on the armrests, then I saunter to the door. Standing behind it, I open it a crack and see that it's a different pizza guy this time. Perfect. Peering around the door, I invite him in. He enters the room and stands in the middle, looking at you sitting immobile in your club chair. I close the door and he turns toward me with a start. He gasps, shocked to see a naked woman standing before him. He quickly averts his eyes and looks back toward you, but you only sit mute and frozen, staring at us both, breathing sharply, watching to see what I plan to do. Soon he realizes you're not going to protest, and I'm not going to run and hide, so he does what he has been aching to do since he set foot in the apartment. He looks at me, with quick sidelong glances at first. Soon he is staring at me full on, eyes sweeping up and down my body, lingering on my breasts and pussy as I smile at him. I shift my weight and arch my back a little, warming under your twin gazes.

After a good long while, I break the spell. I turn toward you and issue a command: "I'll take the pizza into the kitchen; get some money out of my bag." I take the pizza from the guy and make my way slowly to the kitchen. I take my time, exaggerating the sway of my hips, feeling both sets of eyes burning into me. I am becoming aroused by my own power; a fresh wave of juices dampens my inner thighs. In the kitchen I lean over the sink, gasping for breath, feeling the blood pounding in my ears. After I've caught my breath I head back to the living room, where you both wait in silence. My breasts bob as I walk and I thrust them forward, feeling my nipples tighten. I watch you both watching me, and I grin again. Even through your clothes I see both your cocks are rock hard.

I bend over to take the money from you to give to the pizza guy, making sure to give him a good look at everything from behind. As I lean over you, I can tell you are miserable with humiliation, hating to see me reveal myself to a stranger in this way. It's a different game now that I am calling the shots. You grip the money with such force that your knuckles are white. Your head is bowed, your jaw is clenched, and your eyes are squeezed shut. I think I see a tear glinting in the corner of one eye. Yet your cock stays stiff as ever. Before taking the money I touch your forearm, looking into your eyes, studying you to see how much you can take.

You can take it. You open your eyes, relax your grip and hand me the money. I fold a ten-dollar bill and step close to the pizza guy. Heat radiates off my body and rises up between us, the hot musky scent of sex suffusing the narrow space between us. I can hear his breathing quicken, feel his breath on my cheek. "Thanks for coming," I whisper as I slip the bill into his shirt pocket. "Here's a tip."

"It's 'kay, ma'am," he stammers as he follows me to the door. "You already gave me one."

I close the door behind him and turn to you with a smile. "Hungry?" I ask.

The clock chimes the hour and the game is over. I toss on a robe, take your hands and help you to your feet. I wrap my arm around your waist and lead you to the kitchen.

This night is ours.

INK

Jennifer Peters

As Jason reached for the check, I saw the edge of his sleeve peek out from his rolled-up cuffs. The bright colors of the ink caught my eye, and I felt my pussy clench at the sight. There's nothing sexier to me than a well-done work of body art, and Jason was a pretty attractive canvas.

On our first date he'd shown me his arms—each covered in a three-quarter sleeve that stopped just past his elbow—and told me that there were other tattoos, too, but I'd have to wait to see them. "They're hidden," he said, and I smiled. I didn't tell him that night that I had tattoos of my own, also hidden. He'd just have to wait and find out for himself.

I've always been drawn to inked men and started getting my own tattoos when I was twenty-one. But while I appreciate the artistry, I don't like to show off. Every tattoo I have can be hidden under my normal clothing, and it isn't until I know someone well that I show him my ink. Maybe it's because my mother used to call my best friend with the abundance of body art Sideshow Barbie, or maybe it's due to the fact that a date once called tattooed girls "major sluts," but I like to keep my own ink to myself. There's also something extremely personal about each of my works, and I don't always want to share. So until my date gets me naked, I look like your average girl next door. Even Jason, the self-proclaimed tattoo fetishist, had no idea what lay beneath my black cardigan.

By date three I was ready to show him, but he was too well mannered to expect anything. While his tattoos screamed of his rebellious nature, his behavior was anything but. He held doors, pulled out chairs, picked up the tab, said "please" and "thank you," and even called when he said he would. He wasn't the type to rush things and firmly believed in old-fashioned courting. Just my luck. So by date five, I was dying to find his hidden tattoos— and to show him mine.

He paid the bill, left a generous tip, then walked me to his car to take me home. But I decided to take matters into my own hands, and when he reached around me to open my door, I pushed him up against the side of the car and attacked his mouth with my own.

The drive to my house was a blur, and I honestly don't remember the ride. Maybe he sped all the way there, or maybe it just felt that way, but one minute I was sliding into the cramped seat of the small black coupe and in what felt like seconds his hand was reaching into the open door to pull me back out. For the first time, I got the key into the lock and swung the door wide without fumbling, and the stairs to my second-floor apartment went by in a flash. We weren't running; Jason was politely taking his time, looking around and saying ridiculously mundane things about my decorating. Then he turned back to me, standing in the doorway to the living room, pushed me back against the door frame and started to ravage me. He took control of this kiss the way I had our earlier lip-lock against his car, and I moaned into his mouth, loving his sudden show of sexual aggression.

Hands and lips wandered as we kissed, and I waited for the inevitable clothing removal. It took longer than expected—such a gentleman, he was—but eventually his fingers were under my cardigan, my skin tingling with the first gentle touches.

Jason pushed my sweater off my shoulders, leaving me in only a tank top—and baring my arms for the first time. He didn't notice my tattoos at first, my three-quarter sleeves hard to make out in the dim light. It wasn't until he moved to kiss the now-bare skin at the base of my neck that he caught sight of the ink inching up my shoulder. He stilled, his lips pausing only millimeters above my skin, his warm breath tickling me. He lifted the hand that was gripping my forearm and lightly trailed his fingertips along the designs decorating my flesh.

"Beautiful," he mumbled, his lips brushing my shoulder. "Absolutely beautiful."

No one had ever reacted so positively. Men had shown interest, fascination, distaste or indifference. But Jason showed, well, it was almost reverence. He kissed my shoulder, where the ink was artfully faded, his lips burning me and sending flames down my arm all the way through to my fingertips. He kissed down my arm, following the path the flames had burned, and then back up. His mouth crossed my clavicle and moved down my other arm, covering the drawn-on lines with his lips and making me shiver in anticipation. If a few simple kisses on my arms could set me on fire, I couldn't begin to imagine what the rest of the night would bring.

When he reached my shoulder again, his lips lingering for a moment on the faded ink, I felt his fingers tug at the hem of my shirt. I raised my arms and let him pull the shirt up over my head. He tossed the shirt aside, then leaned in and recaptured my lips with his own. His kiss was full of passion, stronger than anything I'd felt from him previously. I had a sneaking suspicion that our shared appreciation of the arts was the cause, and that only made it hotter for me. My fingers danced up his chest until they reached the knot in his tie—so formal, so old-fashioned— and worked it loose, breaking our kiss long enough to pull the silk loop over his head and add it to the small but growing pile of clothing on the floor. Next my fingers found the buttons on his shirt and started to work the small white plastic rounds through their holes. Two inches of material parted as the first button came undone, then two more and again and again as I moved down his chest. I parted the material and pushed it off his shoulders, finally revealing his own sleeves in their entirety, and copied his earlier actions, tracing his artwork with my lips.

I was on fire, and each time I made contact with his flesh, I felt my body flush and my pussy clench. I wanted him, needed him, but there was still more I wanted to share before we crossed that line. I pushed him back and turned him around, moving forward and guiding him to my bedroom from behind. He tried to turn back, to follow, but I wouldn't allow it. I wasn't ready to be so bare in front of him.

In the bedroom, I took charge, and Jason let me. I pushed him down on the bed and leaned over him to unbuckle his belt and get him out of his jeans. I pushed my fingers into the waist-band and gripped the elastic of his underwear, pulling his boxer briefs down with his jeans. I crouched low as I slid his pants off his legs, stopping at his knees when I realized I had yet to take off his shoes and socks. Those items discarded, I continued removing Jason's pants, revealing still more ink.

The more I saw, the more I wanted to show him what I was hiding. Instead, I traced the dragon along his calf, his muscles tensing momentarily under my soft touch. He moaned, almost inaudibly, when I brushed my fingertips along the dragon's scales, and I knew the time was right. I pulled away from Jason's body, stood tall and waited for him to look up at me. When his hazy, hooded eyes met mine, I turned around so my back was to him. I tried to silence my brain as I unzipped my pants and pushed them down, my underwear following after, but I heard his gasp, and the creak of the bedsprings as he sat up to get a closer look.

The wings tattooed on my back are almost always hidden. There's no telling what people will think when they see a grown woman with giant angel wings covering her back, and the comments are rarely positive. So I keep them covered, hiding them from people even after showing them my sleeves, because while I love my ink, I don't have the patience to defend my body art all the time. Showing them off to new people, especially new lovers, always makes me feel vulnerable—naked, even when I'm clothed. Because in addition to the when and how and did it hurt questions, everyone wants to know why, and I don't necessarily want to tell that story every time I take off my clothes.

But Jason didn't ask. He reached, he touched, he traced, but he didn't speak. His fingertips were featherlight against my skin; they sent chills through my body and a wave of heat straight to my pussy. I was readying myself to turn around and face him when his strong arms wrapped around me and twisted my body toward him.

He pulled me in and kissed me, his palms flattening against my back, covering the sketched joints of my wings. It was a simple move, but it conveyed so much to me, and I melted into his arms. I was ready for the next step.

My lips fought his for control of the kiss, but only momentarily; he was in charge. He pulled me in closer and lay back, letting me fall on top of him. I could feel his cock pressing against me, and I shifted closer. While I tried to move so our bodies were tighter together, Jason's hands never stopped running up and down my back, over the wings. His touch made me wet, and I needed him. I needed him to make love to me, to ravage me, to fuck me.

I pushed myself up and properly straddled him, my legs moving to either side of his and my pussy coming to rest directly over his hard cock. From my vantage point, I could see the vivid colors of his tattoos, even in the dim light, and I felt more at ease than I ever had in bed. With Jason's hands pushing firmly against my inked feathers, I guided his cock into me as I sank down onto him.

He filled me completely, or at least it felt that way, as our bodies joined perfectly, like matched pieces from a jigsaw puzzle. I sighed as I sank down farther, to the hilt, my thighs pressing against him, into him, making his flesh and mine indistinguishable from where I sat. I waited, relishing the fullness and the continuous touch of his fingers on my back. Soon, though, his fingertips were burning my skin, and I couldn't sit still. I had to start moving. I shifted up and down, back and forth, slowly riding him. As I got more and more comfortable, my pace picked up, so I was riding him faster and faster. Jason's fingers never stopped caressing my tattoos, his hands moving with the same speed and force as our thrusting bodies, and I'm still not sure if my first climax was due to our sweaty, skin-slapping endeavors or the unbelievably sensuous feeling of his fingertips tracing the inky lines painted over my body.

The release was earth shattering, but it didn't stop there. The sensations only inflamed me further, made me crave even more. I kept moving, and now Jason moved with me, his hips thrusting upward to meet mine, his hands, so gentle before, wrapping around my waist to pull me down to him. I was on fire, and I couldn't stop from taking things further, faster, moving at a fever pitch. I closed my eyes, threw my head back and just moved. I didn't think about what I was doing or how it looked, how I looked; I just moved.

I could feel myself getting closer again, verging on a second climax, and I strove harder to reach it. I wanted it, needed it. But Jason stopped me short.

"Turn around," he commanded, his hands holding me firmly in place when I tried to thrust.

I was so lost in the moment, I didn't hear him at first. He repeated himself. "Turn around." And he started to push at my hips, moving me the way he wanted me.

I didn't understand, but I moved. One leg swung over him, then the other, and then I settled into place again, once more guiding his cock into me. I'd barely gotten into position when Jason started moving inside me. I had to lean forward and grab on to his legs to hold myself steady, but once I had a sense of stability, I began to move with him. And then his hands moved. He gripped my shoulders and stroked his hands up and down my arms, from the faded tops of my sleeves to the vibrant edges halfway down my forearms. As his caresses quickened, so did my thrusts, and I started riding him faster and faster. When his fingers returned to my back, to the outlined layers of feathers, the touch that had set me off initially now caused our fucking to become absolutely frenzied.

I couldn't control myself. Jason's hands on my skin, his soft fingertips brushing over my most cherished artwork, set me off again. I'd never felt more vulnerable or more secure with anyone, and I let go completely. My body quaked, and I could feel my climax in every part of me, from the roots of my hair to the tips of my toes. There wasn't a part of me that wasn't on fire. And when I felt Jason's body trembling beneath me and then felt him coming, one final aftershock went through me, and I shuddered one last time.

Jason's fingers stilled where they were, splayed across my back, and we rested like that a moment, his hands on my wings and one of my hands holding tight to the dragon on his leg, as we caught our breath. When I finally climbed off of him, my body was drenched in sweat and my legs wouldn't stop shaking, but I'd never felt more at peace. I lay down next to him in the bed, rested my head on one tattooed shoulder and reached across him to wrap his other Technicolor arm around me. I fell asleep with his fingers still dancing up and down over my inked feathers. I felt completely naked, and I loved it.

ADORNMENT IS POWER

Teresa Noelle Roberts

Y ou've changed," Joel said. "In a good way," he added hastily. "A hot way."

"You've changed, too. Also in a hot way." Mara assessed her ex quietly, liking what she saw. The cute boy had become a handsome man, the soft, unformed quality she remembered now turned to muscle and confidence. She even liked the streaks of white in his dark brown hair. He probably hated it, but it made him look worldly, mature, like someone who'd take control— or someone worth wrestling for control. "Well, it's been ten years."

"Eleven, but who's counting? You still look like a librarian, but now it's not the shy librarian. Now it's a sexy librarian who's probably not wearing underwear."

"You're just saying that because you found me again on FetLife." He was right about the lack of underwear, but she wasn't going to confirm that—yet. Keep him wondering.

It had been weird running into an ex she'd always carried a

torch for on FetLife, but it had explained a lot. It seemed they were both switches at heart. Back then, before they'd been ready to acknowledge their kinky sides, it had meant a lot of power struggles that eventually ended the relationship.

Now that it was out in the open, though, the power struggles could be...interesting. The people they'd grown into might not be suited to a relationship—that would take time to figure out, though they seemed amazingly compatible over email and the phone—but the sexual tension, now that they were actually in the same room, was probably sending every dog and cat in the neighborhood into heat.

Mara wondered—no doubt he was doing the same thing— who'd take charge first, or if they'd just go for rough, kinky sex the first time with neither of them exactly in charge.

Whether they'd have sex wasn't in question. After all the flirting they'd done long distance, she was amazed they hadn't torn each other's clothes off as soon as he walked into her apartment. At the first kiss, in which they hadn't even bothered with sweet greeting and went straight to devouring, he'd sprung hard in his jeans and ground against her. His scent, his tongue dancing expertly in her mouth, the fantasies they'd teased each other with since they'd found each other again, all conspired to weaken her knees and slick her cunt.

They weren't quite ready to fall into bed, though. No matter how much they'd been flirting and teasing online before setting up an in-the-flesh date, they needed time to adjust to each other's presence, to deal with the fact that the person sitting next to them wasn't one part memory and two parts fantasy, but real.

They'd talked about limits and the like beforehand. What remained to be determined was where the energies of the day were leading, what roles they might fall into. So they were sitting on the couch drinking coffee and making small talk, working up to questions about who might tie up whom tonight.

Their thighs touched. Heat flared between them.

"I never thought I'd see you with a pierced nose." He touched the sapphire stud gently, almost reverently.

She liked the reverence. It helped her decide in which direction things would go.

This time, anyway.

He'd never seen her strong or in charge in the bedroom. Back in college, she'd had fantasies of power and had been pretty tough and take-charge when they had their clothes on. Joel had been her first lover, though, and in the bedroom, she'd been enthusiastic but so shy she had trouble making love with the lights on.

Boy, was he in for a surprise.

"It's not all I have pierced."

Joel raised an eyebrow. "I guess you really have changed. Not so body shy anymore. I'd wondered when all your FetLife pictures were so...clothed. " He ran his gaze up and down her body, reminding her how intimate he'd once been with it and how intimate he'd like to be with it again.

"It keeps the trolls away." Well, that and if she decided to take up with someone she met on the fetish site, she liked the element of surprise. "But you're not a troll." Setting down her coffee cup, she ran her hand over his chest, grazing her nails lightly.

Then, when he purred in appreciation, not so lightly.

"Want to see?"

He nodded. "Oh, yeah."

"Then you will...in good time." She stood, reluctant to pull away from the contact but wanting to move on. "You. In the bedroom. Now. Follow me."

She was gratified by how quickly Joel complied.

Her bedroom, like her fashion sense, appeared staid and classic at first glance. No way an unsuspecting visitor would guess what she kept in the Victorian steamer trunk, and the wrought iron bed frame did a good job of disguising the rings she'd added to it. Joel, though, knowing what he was getting into, obviously noticed the canes among the also-pervertible peacock feathers in the big vase, the suggestive slant of all the artwork. Noticed and grinned at her.

Good to know he was still observant.

Mara perched on the burgundy bedspread, kicking her heels. She'd grabbed a handy crop from the vase in passing, though she hadn't decided if she'd apply it to Joel's undoubtedly fine ass or just use it for effect. "Take off your clothes," she ordered. "Give me a good show."

He grinned and his cock twitched visibly in his jeans.

Slowly and with a little undulating wriggle, he pulled his long-sleeved T-shirt over his head exposing a lightly furred chest, more muscle definition than the last time she'd seen him, and well, she wouldn't call them six-pack abs, but abs that showed he took good care of himself and was staying active. "Nice," she purred, "but too fast. Next time wear a button-down shirt."

"Next time I may be telling *you* what to wear—or not wear. You never know."

That notion started a thrill buzzing in her belly and vibrating her clit, both from the idea that he might take power next time and simply that he was already sure he'd want a next time.

She'd tell him later.

"Now the jeans." He'd already slipped his shoes off.

He peeled those off as slowly and teasingly as he could, revealing simple gray briefs and legs as long and muscled as she remembered. His cock strained at the briefs and that, too, was as lovely as she remembered.

She slipped off the bed and sashayed across the room to him, crop in hand. For a second, less than that, she wished she had one of those stereotyped femme-domme ensembles involving high leather boots and a corset, but a long wool riding skirt, a snug cashmere sweater, flats and high black socks—and the crop—seemed to work just fine for Joel.

She circled him slowly, assessing him without saying a word, occasionally slapping the crop against her own thigh in a way that caused more noise than sting, just to get his attention. She knew from experience on the receiving end how unnerving—and arousing—the silent assessment could be.

By her second circling, his cockhead peeped out the top of his briefs. "Naughty," she said and tapped it with the crop. It made him flinch, then smile—she'd gauged it so it was enough to sting lightly.

Then she set to work in earnest on less delicate areas. He took a deep breath as she smacked the crop against his flat stomach, then let it out with obvious pleasure. He bit his lips most gratifyingly as she worked over his thighs. His hips strained forward at each blow, as if he imagined fucking her while she beat him. (A hot notion and yeah, she'd like to try the cropping and fucking combination, too, though whether she'd prefer to be the cropper or the croppee would depend on her mood.)

And when she worked her way around to his ass, he let out a delicious sigh before she even got started.

She yanked his briefs off unceremoniously. "Lovely," she said, running her hand over the firm, graspable curve. This was the male body at its best, with hard muscle under deliciously soft, touchable skin.

She caressed. She dug in her nails. She spanked a few times, until it became obvious her hand would get sore long before Joel's ass did.

She pointed to the bed. "Bend over," she ordered. "Put your hands on the bed." She flashed to the college dorm room and him saying the same words to her. Back then, she was so young and inexperienced that being fucked from behind in that position seemed terribly embarrassing and kinky, and the command in his words had raised her hackles and melted her defenses at the same time.

She wondered if he remembered, too, and if he got the same thrill at the tables being turned.

She could *really* turn the tables if she wanted to. She had a strap-on in the toy box, and the view of him bent over in surrender, ass thrust out, made that image awfully tempting.

Another time, maybe. That wasn't a fantasy they'd discussed yet. She wouldn't be surprised if he'd go for it, but it didn't seem like something to spring on a guy. If nothing else, payback would be a bitch.

Instead, she turned the crop on him, smacking away on this more padded area. He yelped a couple of times and pulled away—but instantly stuck his now pink-splotched butt out for more.

It wasn't the act of hitting a guy, of inflicting pleasurable pain that turned Mara on most when she topped. She liked it, sure, but what made her wet and made her cunt twitch were Joel's reactions, the small, strained noises he made, the way he couldn't decide whether to flinch away or push back for more, the way he ground against the bed when she gave him a chance, his aching cock eager to fuck something, if only the bedspread.

Mara knew how he felt. Her clit was swollen, so tender even the air on it felt like a caress, and her cunt ached to be filled.

What was she waiting for, then?

She pulled the crop back and struck hard at the sweet spot

where ass met thigh, hitting more with the flexible shaft than the leather flat.

He let out a woof that was half surprise, half pleasured pain. Two times more she striped him—the marks probably wouldn't stay, but they looked pretty now. She ran her fingernails over the welts, making him shiver.

"Up on the bed," she ordered. "On your back."

He obeyed so quickly she swore he'd teleported.

She grabbed a condom from the bedside table. She teased the length of his shaft with her fingernails, loving the way his body shuddered. Then, trying to conceal that her own hands were shaking with need, she sheathed him.

She needed that in her and she needed it about five minutes ago.

She reached for the zipper of her skirt.

Then she changed her mind.

When they'd been a couple, he'd been the one to cajole and command her out of her clothes. Then, being young and not too experienced himself, half the time he'd gotten so excited he hadn't bothered doing more than unzipping his jeans. She wasn't shy anymore, but it wouldn't hurt to remind him that the balance of power wasn't what it used to be and, at least for tonight, the ball was in her court.

Mara kicked off her shoes, hiked up her skirt and straddled his hips, letting the skirt down again to conceal her body.

She circled the base of his cock with one hand, raised her hips and lowered herself onto him.

She'd had her share of cocks inside her in the past decade and had enjoyed them all. Joel's had been the first, though. She hadn't realized until he was fully sheathed in her that she'd had a romantic notion that fucking him would feel like coming home.

No. Not really.

They weren't the same people they were back then, and his cock, his whole body, felt new and exciting rather than familiar. No, fucking him didn't feel like coming home—but it certainly made her feel like coming and a lot faster and harder than it had back on Round One. She'd enjoyed sex then, but it had still been new and awkward, her orgasms erratic.

Knowledge is power. And power is hot.

She began to move, riding Joel as mercilessly as he'd once ridden her.

He groaned. His hands fisted in the bedding so he wouldn't grab her hips and try to control the rhythm, she guessed. Good boy. Someone had trained him well.

But she wanted his hands on her—on her terms. Two months of teasing as they got to know each other again had led up to today, and she was running out of patience.

She grabbed his right hand, slid it under her skirt and put it where she needed it. "There's one of those piercings you talked about," he said, his voice breathy. "Right in your hood."

"Yes. Did you feel the others?" She ground down, giving him a hint.

"Oh, yeah. Outer labia?"

"Inner, too."

"May I see? Please?"

"Not yet. Right now, use Braille."

He reached down, stroking the stretched flesh where he filled her, stroking the three rings on each lip. "My god."

It was getting harder to talk, but she managed to push out, "You could say that. Please...get back to my clit. I'm getting close."

He complied. "So am I. I'm afraid once you start coming..."

She supposed she should do the toppy thing and threaten him with dire consequences if he came too soon—but when she played on the bottom, that sort of threat pushed her right over the edge.

Besides, it was a thrill to feel irresistible.

"Do it," she said, amazed by how strong and confident her voice sounded when she was ready to melt all over him.

He obeyed.

She raked her fingernails down his chest as she came, and that, or her contractions or both culminated the long tease as he exploded.

It wasn't until much later—she thought they'd both dozed off with her sprawled on top of him—that Joel said, "You still have clothes on."

She laughed. "I know that. That was deliberate."

"I thought it might be. Making a point about the way things used to be?"

"Maybe." She plucked at his nipple with her nails until he batted her hand away. "Or maybe it's just that adornment is power."

"Naked can be powerful, too. Please…I want to see you, Mara. Want to see what I was feeling. I promise I won't touch."

Her body stirred again, brought to life by the need in his voice and the power she had over him.

Hell, she could taunt him with the prospect of her naked body and keep denying him indefinitely, or at least until he decided he'd had enough of the game and turned top on her. And that would be fun, too.

Instead, she slithered off the bed.

She peeled off the sweater, turned so he could see the tattooed jungle scene, complete with leopard, that covered much of her back. She removed her bra while she was turned away, then faced him again, displaying large nipple rings and a spray of roses tattooed on her left breast.

"Your mom?" His voice was hesitant. Her mother—Rose— had been diagnosed with breast cancer while they were dating the first time.

"Alive and kicking. This was in honor of five years of remission, though she'd flip if she knew I'd done it."

She unzipped the skirt and let it slither to the floor. She could feel him counting: belly button ring; knotwork around the navel; a snake, only its green head visible above her long black socks; a bar in her shaved pubic mound; the clit hood piercing.

She let him get a good look, then rolled the socks off. One leg was wrapped with the snake, the other still bare.

She knew what he was most curious about, though. She used her fingers to open her lips, showing off the piercings Joel had touched without seeing.

He leaned forward, getting as close as he could without getting off the bed. His muscles were strained, bunched under the skin, and he gripped the bedspread so hard his knuckles were white. But he was being good, keeping his word, not touching.

"I used to feel too exposed without my clothes on," Mara said. "You did your best to make me feel good about my body, and you helped a lot. But I guess I needed to do it my own way—to find a way I wouldn't feel so naked being naked."

"After all, adornment is power," he quoted her.

"And I'm always adorned, so I always have power. Even if I decide not to use it for a while." She strode over, within easy reach. "Speaking of which, remember how you promised not to touch?"

He nodded, obviously not sure how the game might be shifting.

"Forget that promise. And Joel—don't be gentle."

MUSCLE BOUND

K. D. Grace

When I trained with Becky Strauss, Rachel McLish had just bared her well-muscled, feminine body in her book, *Flex Appeal*. Arnold Schwarzenegger was still *Conan the Barbarian*, and his lovely but savage sidekick, Sandahl Bergman, was wielding her badass sword with arms that were the envy of every woman.

I had just finished university and was working at a local radio station in Central Oregon. My refrigerator was covered with pictures of women with washboard abs and granite thighs. But books and magazine articles were no substitute for experience, so I scraped together the money to join Muscle Bound Health Club.

Becky Strauss taught women's weight training at Muscle Bound to supplement an artist's meager income. I wouldn't recognize her from the glammed-up photos I see of her today. But her face wasn't what I was looking at then. It was her body that captivated me.

"You're very strong," she said as I grunted out five squats in rapid succession. "You've never lifted weights before?"

"I was raised on a farm," I stammered. "I've been lifting weights all my life."

She chuckled. The sexy, but can-do contralto of her voice was a puff of warm air against my shoulder. "I grew up in Kansas. Guess it comes naturally for us farm girls."

When I finished the set, she rested a large hand on my back. "Good job. Now you can be my spotter. Listen up, everyone, and pay attention," she called out to the rest of the group. Becky was nearly six feet tall with miles of rock-solid legs well displayed in workout shorts, and I got a great view as she stood in front of me and positioned herself under the barbell. "Spotting is especially important when you're doing squats. Your partner's safety is in your hands. Remember that."

The other women gathered round to watch as Becky took the barbell across her shoulders and explained about keeping the spine straight and the head up. All the while I admired the narrowing of her back, the curve of her hips and the way her butt pressed against the satin fabric of her shorts like two halves of an opened peach. Even in my heavy-duty sports bra, my nipples ached at the sight.

That first day I was torn between the excitement of finally getting to work seriously with free weights and admiring the powerful physicality of Becky Strauss. Becky's breasts were small and firm and she never wore a bra. When she demonstrated flies on the incline bench, I could barely breathe from the sight of her. The working muscle groups were completely visible beneath the spaghetti-strapped leotard she wore. I held my breath as she lifted the dumbbells in an arc in front of her chest. The motion compressed her striated pectorals, forcing her lovely small breasts to rise to exquisite prominence with each press of the dumbbells. All the while, her nipples were like two large pearls straining just beneath the caress of Lycra.

That night, I masturbated thinking about the two of us alone in the gym doing squats. In my fantasy, she kept adding more weight to my barbell, always complimenting my strength as I strained upward beneath the load. I imagined her sliding down my shorts and panties to watch my glutes at work. I imagined thrusting my butt out, keeping my back straight just like she had instructed. I imagined her watching, admiring, coaching. And when I was at the bottom of my squat, just when I was straining under the weight for the upward thrust, I imagined her making me hold that position until I could feel my pulse throbbing in my cunt.

While I strained, I imagined her sliding her fingers between my pussy lips to find me slick and ready. My moans and grunts were as much from her explorations as from the weight bearing down on me. Then at last I imagined her helping me lift the barbell back onto the rack and rewarding my efforts by slipping the leotard off over her shoulders and letting me touch her breasts and thumb her hard nipples.

I came then and slept, dreaming of Becky Strauss.

The class met twice a week, but I came in early, stayed late and worked out extra on my own, always in hopes of spending a few more minutes with Becky.

One evening after a particularly hard leg workout, I went to the sauna. The heat was just beginning to dissipate the tension in my quads and glutes when the door opened and Becky stepped inside.

"Good workout today, Kate." She dropped her towel. Surely I must have stared. What else could I have done? The plane of her belly stretched supple and flat between the rise of her breasts and the closely trimmed curls shielding her pubis—both places I visited regularly in my fantasies. She dropped onto the bench opposite me, positioning herself so her back was against the cedar wall and her legs stretched out on the wooden slats in front of us, her toes nearly touching mine.

As she shifted to get comfortable, moaning softly in the muscle-relaxing heat, I glimpsed the pale pink folds of her pussy, and for a moment, the world seemed slightly out of sync, just enough to let me memorize the soft pout of heavy folds, the brief peek at her dark anus and the moist intimations of her clit pressing out from under its hood. I collected that moment, along with so many other moments spent with Becky and filed them all away in my imagination, to be used whenever I chose, for my private pleasuring.

I squirmed to get comfortable, blushing until I was sure my face was glowing, awkwardly rearranging myself, desperate, for some reason, that she should have a glimpse of me as well. I felt foolish and feminine and horny all at the same time, and I didn't know what to do about it. But before I could make too big a fool of myself, Becky spoke.

"I can't believe the class is nearly over."

"Me, neither," I breathed.

"What are you going to do?" she asked. "There won't be an advanced class until the fall, and you're too skilled to repeat the beginning course."

"I'll work out on my own I guess. But I'll come to the class anyway, you know, to make sure I'm doing things right." More importantly, I'd come to class to be near her, I thought.

She studied me until I began to feel uncomfortable, then she spoke. "I need a training partner, Kate, and you need a challenge. I think you're ready if you're interested."

After that, we trained together three or four times a week. I was in heaven, surrounded by the sage smell of her sweat and the tangy underlying scent that I knew to be something even wetter, even sweeter. We declared war on our abs, we did flies until we could barely lift our arms, we piled the weight on the barbell and did squats until our legs trembled. Sometimes we had a sauna, sometimes we went out to eat after, but always, at night it was Becky Strauss I visited in my fantasies.

One day, she called and asked if I was free for a late lunch at Mountain View Café. I thought she sounded a bit strange. Still, if I was going to be with Becky, I wanted to look my best. I took my time getting ready, making sure my makeup was perfect and my jeans were the ones that accentuated my curves—muscular curves that she had admired. I wore a summer sweater with a plunging neckline showing off my hard-earned pecs along with a bit of my deep cleavage.

She was already there when I arrived.

Once the waitress had brought two hibiscus iced teas and left to refill the condiments after the lunch rush, Becky spoke without preamble. "I fucked my ex last night."

"Oh?" My pulse accelerated. Becky wasn't shy about sharing, and the opportunist in me figured I'd be masturbating to the details of her sex life tonight.

"He was just passing through, seeing to the shipping of a couple of paintings his firm bought from me. He always liked my work," she added. "He asked me for dinner and drinks and one thing led to another." She waved her hand absently. "It was a mistake, of course, but not really such a bad thing. It's good to know that I made the right choice in divorcing him."

"I'm glad."

"Nothing has really changed. All the things I hated about him when we were married are still there."

"Oh?"

She took a contemplative drink of her tea, and we both paused as the waitress brought our salads. Then she spoke, leaning over the table, holding my gaze. "Sex is not his forte. I got tired of finishing myself off in the bathroom afterward."

I nearly choked on my tea.

"I hope I'm not embarrassing you, Kate. I just needed someone to talk to. Don't get me wrong, I'm not upset. In fact, I feel like I've just had a revelation. I mean, I've been celibate now for almost two years, and it's not so bad. Anyway, it's not just the sex. I mean, if it was just that, I could live with the masturbating afterward, but I'm thirty years old. I'm not getting any younger. If I'm ever going to make my art work for me, the time's now. I'm not cut out for a house in the suburbs and the kids and..." Her voice trailed off and she stared into her tea. The silence stretched between us, and I was about to break it with some awkward cliché about following one's dream, when she saved me the trouble and spoke. "Right now it's just beginning to be what I'd always hoped it would be. I have several commissions to work on. I've got my classes and my training. I'm doing all right." She nodded hard and squared her shoulders. "Last night just confirms I made the right choice."

Not knowing what else to say, I raised my tea glass. "Here's to right choices."

"To right choices," she returned the toast.

We talked about sex and weight training and our plans for the future. Mostly we talked about sex. We stayed until the waitress began glancing at the clock, then back at our table. The dinner crowd was just trickling in when we paid the tab and headed out into the warm evening. I can't remember now exactly how it happened, but we ended up at her house.

She lived in a rented Victorian on the edge of town, way too big for one person and way too rundown to qualify as anything but a fixer-upper. "An artist needs lots of space," she said, as she gave me the grand tour. "And so does a bodybuilder. I have space for my weights, my books and my bike and my skis. It's good for me."

The décor was hippie retro. The walls that weren't painted in murals best described as Renaissance nouveau were lined with brick and raw lumber bookshelves loaded down with everything from Nietzsche to herbal medicine to graphic novels, all half hidden in a jungle of overgrown houseplants.

In the living room, we plopped down on a huge pile of cushions in the middle of the green shag carpet. She opened a bottle of expensive chardonnay one of her wealthier clients had given her as a bonus for a family portrait. Once we had properly admired the elderflower bouquet and the slight butterscotch undertones of the wine, I grabbed Becky's dog-eared copy of *Flex Appeal* from the bookshelf and began to flip through it. Becky scooted closer to look on. I flipped the page, and we found ourselves looking down at a bikini-clad Rachel McLish posing to best display hard bronze muscles overlaid by just enough feminine softness that no one could ever imagine she was anything but one-hundred-percent primo woman.

"You remind me of her," Becky said, pushing my hair off my shoulder and behind my ear.

My heart skipped a beat. "Me? You're kidding, right? I'm too dumpy, I have no butt, and my—"

She stopped my words with a finger against my lips. "Every time I see you in the sauna, I think of how much you remind me of her." She scooted a little closer, and I could almost taste the wine on her breath. "Your breasts are bigger," she peeked down the front of my sweater and offered me a teasing smile. "I like 'em bigger."

"Really? You like them?" I looked down and cupped my tits.

"I always wished I had smaller breasts, more like yours."

"Come on," She grabbed my hand and pulled me to my feet. "Bring the book. Let's practice a little posing." She pulled me into a room with stripped wood floors, a training bench and a fairly basic, if high-quality, set of free weights. All the walls were mirrored ceiling to floor.

"I ate a lot of peanut butter to pay for this," she said when she heard my gasp of approval. "But it's been worth the sacrifice." She sat the wineglass on the bench, and before I knew what was happening, she had pulled her shirt off over her head, followed in short order by jeans and pale blue panties. I watched as she struck the same pose Rachel McLish held in the photo. "What do you think?" she called over her shoulder.

"Nice definition in the delts and hamstrings," I replied, too shy to tell her it was her breasts I was actually admiring.

"Really? My thighs don't look flabby?" She flexed harder.

"I don't see any flab anywhere." My reply was breathless, as it always was when I saw her naked. I stood shyly at the door with my arms folded protectively across my breasts, which ached with the heavy fullness I felt for the same reason.

She studied herself in the mirror, turning slightly from side to side. "Of course I can't do the tit thing like she can." She turned to face me, giving me a full frontal view that made me feel like my cunt was bathed in champagne. "Come on. Show me how women with tits do it." She laughed out loud. "Don't be shy. I've seen your tits before and your pussy. Don't think I didn't notice how you flash me in the sauna."

"I don't."

"Of course you do." She reached for my jeans and gave them a tug. "Here, let me help."

I slapped her hands away, but she was too fast. With a movement any adolescent boy would have envied, she reached under my blouse and unhooked my bra with a resounding snap of elastic. I yelped.

"Come on, I want to see you pose, and you can't pose in all these clothes." Her voice became singsongy as she tugged the sweater over my head until it covered my face and bound my arms, leaving me blindfolded and trapped at her tender mercy. Then she went to work on my jeans. "I wanna see you po-ose, get rid of all these clo-othes," she sang between breathless giggles, tugging and pulling until my jeans and panties were down around my ankles, and I was bound by them at one end and my sweater and bra at the other.

I gasped and jumped as I felt her warm lips against my navel, then between my breasts. Her strong hands moved up my ribs to cup me. "Mmm, if I had these, I wouldn't be able to keep my hands off myself." I felt her humid breath against my ear. "Tell you a secret, Katie. Last night while Derek was fucking me"—with one hard shove she freed me of the cumbersome upper-body wear, and I found myself almost nose to nose with her, staring into her large brown eyes—"It was thinking about you that made me come."

She reached down to help me free my legs from my jeans. "I think about you a lot when I come." She kissed my earlobe, then my cheek. "I love the way your pecs tense and your breasts mound up when you do flies. I love the way your quads bulge and the way your pussy presses against your shorts when you're doing heavy squats. And when you finish a hard set, I love to listen to you breathe." Her lips brushed mine. "I imagine that's what you sound like when you've just come."

I returned her kiss, timidly at first.

It was as though I had given her permission. She ate my mouth with a hunger that I returned in kind. All the while she walked me, pushed me, pressed me, until my butt and shoulders were squished hard against the cold mirrored wall, and I sucked in my breath at the shock of it. Then she drenched my breasts in warm wet kisses, pinching my nipples to sharp little points and tugging them none too gently with her teeth. She growled, and I mewled like a kitten, soaking myself, guiding her hand over my mound between my unsteady thighs. I bore down and rode her palm until her whole hand was slippery, and the room smelled of female heat.

"I've never been with a woman before." It sounded foolish the second I said it.

"Neither have I." She brought her wet hand away from my cunt to her lips, then her pink tongue flicked over her fingertips. "Taste how yummy you are." She offered me two fingers like nipples, and I dutifully sucked and licked. Then she pulled away and with a hard shove, turned me so my cheek and tits were against the mirror, forcing the breath from me in steamy clouds on the glass. My nipples tingled from the chill.

With a grunt, she pressed her whole body tight against me, and I was sandwiched between her and the mirror. "I want a print of you." She shifted and insinuated until I could barely breathe from the press. "You know what I mean, a print like an ink-block print." Her body undulated against mine until I was so hot from the feel of her that I humped the mirror, relishing the cold hardness of it against my pubis.

She forced my legs apart with a knee, then knelt and began to nibble and tug at my labia, still holding me tight against the mirror. She teased my clit until the weight of it felt heavier than anything I'd lifted on the barbells. Then, with a slurp, she pulled away. "Turn around one more time."

I did as she commanded.

"That's a girl, now bend over. Spread your legs just a little more. Keep them straight, that's right. Now look."

Bent practically double, I looked down between my legs into the mirror at the view of my pussy like I'd never seen it before, slick and heavily swollen, the normal pink color darkened to the purple-red of arousal. The whole of my vulva pouted like a hungry mouth, crowned by the hard marble erection of my clit.

Still kneeling, taking in the view of me, Becky suckled each of my breasts in turn, then pushed me back, moving me, arranging me, shifting and lifting my buttocks until every bit of my cunt was pressed against the mirror. The pressure of her hand against my pubis and the cold hardness of the mirror was all it took to send me over the edge.

I stumbled forward and fell against her with the intensity of my orgasm. As she tumbled backward onto the floor, I wrapped myself around her, groping her everywhere I could reach with my mouth and my hands. I nipped her breasts, I stroked her curls, I probed her pussy with my fingers, amazed at the strength of her grip. We were all over each other, tasting, touching, testing, then doing it all again. We explored and experimented until everything was spent. Consciousness slipped away, and we slept.

It was long toward morning when she woke me. Moonlight drenched the room. We had fallen asleep in the corner on an exercise mat. "You have to see this," she whispered as she pulled me to my feet. In my drowsiness, I half stumbled, half followed as she led me to stand in front of the mirror.

"Look, I have a print of you coming."

And sure enough, the moonlit mirror told the story of my arousal. There, pressed against the glass, were the half-dome prints of my buttocks, the curve of my back, the press of my shoulders. To the right was the peach and rose smear of my makeup where my cheek had been. And below that, amazingly clear, if slightly flattened and distorted, was the image of my breasts, nipples and areolas clearly visible, captured in the medium of Becky's warm saliva. Beneath was the press of my belly, the stipple brush marks of my pubic curls and the swell of my thighs. But the true masterpiece was next to it. There in the medium of my own juices, spread and splayed with exquisite detail right down to the nub of my clit, was my pussy.

"Look." She took my hand and pulled me closer to inspect the shape of myself on the mirror. "See how the muscles seem to be in motion, almost like there are little waves rising from beneath the surface. That's what an orgasm looks like. That's what your orgasm looks like."

I'm not an artist, so I don't know the technique Becky used, though she did try to explain it to me. What I do know is that life-size prints of my orgasming pussy and my other *Mirror Images*, as Becky entitled the series inspired by that night's passion, presently hang in some of the wealthiest homes in the Northwest. I understand any one of them is now worth more than I make in a year. Knowing that I get to be an exhibitionist vicariously to the wealthy does strange things to my head—and to my cunt.

I read glowing reviews of Becky's latest exhibitions in New York and London, but I've not seen her in years. She gave me one of the first prints of my orgasming cunt as a gift for my inspiration. It still hangs over my bed. I suppose I could always sell it if times get tough. But I like that unique view of myself and the memories attached. I've always been sentimental, and after all, it was Becky who made me come—many more times than she actually knows about or was present for. And it was Becky who made my pussy into a work of art. That being said, I think I'll keep the print above my bed right where it is.

SHOWER
FITTINGS

Giselle Renarde

The steam caressed Michelle's caramel flesh like wafting rose-scented clouds, rising and dissipating into the white of the ceiling. Warm water pelted her chest, tempting her nipples to peak in readiness for Sterling's touch. He stepped into the shower all man, his muscular abs gleaming even before the water kissed their perfect contours.

Her drenched nakedness called his cock to arms, ready for the war games, the friendly fire. Extending her hand in peace, she pulled him to her until her tits met his hard front. She kissed his chest, his neck, his full lips under the welcome assault of the shower like falling rain. All the while, she pumped his cock. She could never bring herself to tug him hard like he asked for. How could that feel good? No, her style was gentle all the way, slow and steady like Aesop always said.

Sterling grabbed her ass and squeezed. When he drew breath to speak, she knew what to expect. He'd noticed the effects of the cardio classes at the gym and the jogging three times a week.

It was tough some mornings, getting up at six, but the results were well worth the effort.

"Hard to believe this thing's one-hundred-percent fiberglass," he said.

Pardon me?

Pulling away to look her husband in the eye, Michelle asked, "Baby, what'd you just call me?"

Without hearing her—or at least, without responding directly to her question—Sterling fondled the shower wall. "It's all one piece. Isn't that incredible? The tub, the wall, all the way up to the ceiling, it's just one big molded sheet of fiberglass."

Michelle rolled her eyes, not entirely amused, but not entirely put off. She circled her arms around him. "Honey-cake, while you're going on and on *about* the shower, you are one-hundred-percent forgetting about the woman *in* the shower." She planted kisses across his chest. "*Naked* in the shower." Kissing up his neck to nibble at his ear, she teased, "You got your precious shower fittings, now how about fitting your precious wife with that big ol' cock, hmm?"

Sterling growled as she swiped his cockhead across her belly. It felt good, but the sensation would be better with suds.

As she reached for the soap, Michelle's heel backed into an invisible pool of dried shampoo from the nearly empty upside-down bottle on the tub's ledge. She started to slip. She reached for the wall, but of course that was no help. The wall was solid and smooth. As she lost her balance, slipping backward, Sterling tightened his grip around her waist and pulled her to his chest.

It happened so fast she didn't even get a chance to shriek in terror, but it was enough to set her straight. Clinging to her husband's firm black body, she cried, "I knew it. What did I tell you? I knew it. Didn't I say?"

"You're okay," he consoled, like she was a child fallen from a bicycle. "I've got you in my arms. You're okay."

"I am most certainly not okay," she said, releasing him to loosen the pool of dried shampoo with her big toe. Picking up the upside-down bottle, she squeezed its contents into her palm before replacing it, right side up, on the tub ledge. She forced the jasmine-scented shampoo into her hair. "All our marriage, you want one thing. You want to do me in the shower. I've done everything—*everything*—else there is to do because, let's face it, I'm no prude. Still, all I hear from you is *shower, shower, shower*. I don't want to do it in the shower, Sterling. I don't feel safe. I could fall asleep and break my neck. Still, all I hear…"

"You're worried you might fall asleep in the shower?" Sterling interrupted. A tentative grin broke like a rainbow across his lips.

Had she misspoken? Yes, she had. She could laugh it off and kiss his lips, then his cock…*and wind up smashing her head open on the faucet?* No way. She had no mercy at times like these. "Fall and slip," I said. "Not fall asleep. You'd better clean those big ears when you're done with that big…"

Her gaze had fallen to the danger zone. She couldn't resist her husband's cock, any time, any place. The temptation was right there, close enough to touch. *But no.* Not safe.

"Hey, what'd my big ears ever do to you?" he chuckled, running his hands down her backside.

His hard body exerted such a pull on her. "Hmm? What'd you say?"

"Maybe you ought to clean your ears out, too, girl," he laughed, tracing a soapy palm along his shaft. He knew she would watch if he did. Of course she would watch. That bad boy was spectacular. "You seem a little…distracted?"

"Hmm?" she repeated. He stroked it root to tip, letting his cockhead fall from his fingers just as the other hand prepared to catch it. A sly grin spread across his lips as he watched her watch him.

Without so much as rinsing her hair, Michelle grabbed hold of Sterling's cock. When she pushed the shower curtain aside, he followed her to the bedroom. Her husband was like a dog so happy for its walk, it overlooks the leash it's on.

"Girl, you must be hungry for it. You didn't even turn the water off!" he chuckled. She'd fallen so deep into lust that economic and environmental concerns had escaped her.

"Oh," she replied, almost like she might do something about that. She didn't. Instead, she pushed his dripping-wet body down on the ottoman that used to match the dark green velvet chair. Now the chair was gone and the ottoman didn't match anything, but they still found use for it.

He sat, leaning back, hands gripping the ottoman. His cock pointed to Michelle like a dowsing rod. *I found the juice*, it said. *Mighty wet down there. Refresh yourself in that water, man. It's all for you.*

With shampoo dripping down her shoulders, Michelle climbed on board. She straddled her man—one knee on the ottoman, one foot on the floor—and heaved her body down on him. She wasn't heavy, but he sure knew she was there. Her cunt was all around him, soaking and stroking his cock. When she moved on him, he moved in her. As she bounced and heaved, her tits swung before him like caramel temptations.

Holding the small of her back, Sterling curled toward her chest as she rose like an angel and fell like a demon. When he took her tits in his mouth and sucked those finest of nipples, she sighed his name. She proclaimed that she loved him...or she loved *that*.... She loved *something*, anyway, and something's better than nothing.

As Sterling sucked, she bounced faster, gearing up for the

explosion that was soon to come. She could feel it right down to her toes. That big cock did it for her every time. Working her tits was a nice touch—showed the man cared—but Michelle knew she could come with no other encouragement than his cock in her pussy and the sound of wet thighs slapping.

He came before she did. She could see it in the magical contortions of his face, the way his lips twitched and his eyes rolled back in his head like he was having some kind of seizure. She wasn't far behind. She was sure she looked like a million bucks when she had her orgasm. Of course, she never dared to glance over at the mirror when the time to come came, just in case she was wrong. Sometimes it was more pleasant living the lie.

Lifting her from the ottoman, cock in cunt, Sterling carried Michelle into the bathroom. She chuckled and called him crazy as he leaned her head under the running water to wash out her shampoo.

"Reach over slowly and close the taps," he said.

She looked up at him like he had three heads. "You have got to be kidding me. I can't do that. I'll crack my skull."

"Trust me. I've got you," he whispered in that voice like dark velvet. "Anyway, it's just fiberglass. You might bump your head, but you're not going to crack anything."

"Very reassuring," she replied, pushing her voice flat. The taps really weren't that far away. She reached out and shut them off quick as a bunny. Something bubbled inside her, and she looked up at Sterling in amazement. "I did it!"

"See?" he said, pulling her to his chest. She grabbed a towel as he carried her from the bathroom to the bedroom and tossed her onto the satin coverlet. She bounced against the mattress and chuckled in adoration. He kissed her legs. Crawling up her body, he said, "Nothing to be afraid of, except maybe that you'll like it too much."

Wrapping the towel around her wet hair, she laughed like it was unfathomable she'd ever enjoy shower sex. But he was right. She might like it. She might love it. If she tried.

"It's not that I don't *want* to, honey-cake," she began. He crawled up to her chest, resting his cheek on her breast and his body next to hers. "You know what I'm like. I want everything."

"I know you do," he chimed in with a deep chuckle.

"And it's not to spite you, though I know it may look that way."

"I know it's not."

"The simple cause is I'm afraid of getting hurt. That's it," she went on, trying to convince herself.

"I believe you," he began. Cautiously, he admitted, "I didn't at first. That's why I got that rusted-out old turquoise tub replaced by the new one. I figured you didn't appreciate the surroundings."

"Surroundings don't trouble me," she teased. Stretching her hands above her head, she flexed her feet. "I never seemed to mind getting it on in that rusted-out old turquoise car you used to have."

He wouldn't let her get the better of him. Pinching her sides, he replied, "I never had any rusted-out turquoise car and you know it."

"Oh," she taunted, pinching him back. "Well, then, who am I thinking of?" She laughed, giving away the ruse. He chuckled right along with her until exhaustion overtook him.

As his dark lids closed, she saw in him the twenty-two-year-old she'd met in college. Though it wasn't long ago, it seemed like a different era altogether. They'd been so polite with each other in the beginning—almost to the point of formality at times—like belles and beaux of the Regency period. Not that a man and woman branded with their skin tones would have been wearing suits and gowns or courting at debutante balls back then. Maybe that was the appeal. They wanted what their ancestors couldn't have.

She would have done anything for him back then. He would have done anything for her, too, but he would still do anything for her, so nothing had changed there. One evening, long before they were married, they were chatting each other up on the phone. Sterling mentioned having a hankering for a certain brand of potato chips. Well, the second they hung up that phone, didn't she head right out to buy him a bag? Not just that, but hand-deliver it right to his door? She did, indeed. A kind man deserved his just reward.

Now she took him for granted, she realized. Every morning, he'd be there beside her as she woke up. Every night he'd be there, too. She could count on all that, so why bother working for it? *Why bother?* What kind of lazy cow had she become in only six years of marriage? A kind man deserved his reward, as much now as ever. And was Sterling a kind man? Sure he was. If she was planning on spending her whole marriage in a lethargic rut, she might as well give up on it right this minute.

"There is one shower that might be suited to your purpose," Michelle said.

Stirring, he rolled his head from her breast to the mattress. He'd been close to snoring. "What was that you said, baby girl?"

"You remember in the spring a whole bunch of us girls went up to Sarah's summer house for the weekend?"

Who did they know with a summer house, aside from his parents? "Who do we know called Sarah?"

"White girl from the gym?" Michelle jogged his memory. "Won all that money in a settlement? Right away bought that big house on the Path and a summer house by the lake? Remember?"

"Oh, yeah, Settlement Sarah," Sterling chuckled. Picking up his wife's hand, he kissed her wrist. "Why didn't you say so?"

Michelle chuckled, too, shaking her head. "Anyway, doesn't so much matter who she is. What's more important is the shower she's got at that summer house." Smiling wide, she flipped to her side and slithered down the bed until she and Sterling were face-to-face. She rubbed the towel against her hair one last time before tossing it on the sopping wet ottoman. "I think you'd like that shower. Big-time."

Kissing her pink lips, Sterling put on his coyest tone. "And why would I like it so much?"

"Because," she replied, returning the kiss. "It's the one shower I can think of where we could get it on without me being afraid of breaking my neck."

Circling an arm around his wife's waist, he growled, "I like the sound of that. But what's so special about her shower?"

"We'll go there," she offered, sitting up in a hurry. "I'll show you."

Sterling shook his head. "It's all pie in the sky unless Settlement Sarah loans you the keys."

"No need," she cheered, beaming like a kid with an ice cream. "Keys are in the hollow turtle." She pulled open the top dresser drawer, and took out a nice lacy white pair of undies and the matching bra. "Sarah's in Costa Rica. No end to that settlement money. I'm sure she won't mind if we make it a day trip. Better that someone gets some use out of the place."

Climbing out of bed to collect the wet towel from the ottoman, he said, "You can't just invite yourself to somebody's summer house while she's out of the country. Where are your manners, girl?"

"Oh, so you're my daddy now, are you?" she laughed, throwing on a summer dress. Handing him a clean polo shirt, shorts and underwear, she went on, "Well then, Daddy Sterling, how's about taking me up to that summer house for a romp in the shower?"

He considered her through smiling eyes before agreeing. Outwardly, he came off as reluctant, but that was just to show Michelle this wasn't the sort of thing he considered right and good. Inwardly, he was dancing.

The summer house looked familiar, somehow. Michelle must have showed him pictures from her girls' weekend. Or maybe it simply epitomized all that was luxury in a contemporary lake house. It was situated on a small inlet overlooking a lake mirroring trees on every shore.

But they hadn't driven all the way to the Kawarthas for the scenery.

"Bathroom's this way," Michelle said, setting the latchkey down on the hall table.

Sterling followed her up the stairs. "In my day, a cabin was a shack. You were lucky to have someplace to escape to in the hot months and luckier still if that place had bedrooms. Just look at my parents' old summer escape."

"Yeah, one big room with a curtain separating the sleeping area from the kitchen," she chuckled.

"And back when my grandparents bought it, all those cabins up there were the same way. They were the first black…"

"I know, I know," Michelle smirked. "First black family on the whole lake."

"I guess you've heard all my stories now," Sterling sighed, throwing his arms around her. From behind, he grabbed her breasts and gave them a good squeeze.

"About a million times, I'd say."

Releasing her tits, he gave her a smack on the ass to lead on. "I still say all this luxury is overkill. We've got luxuries in the city. I come out to the woods, to the lake, to commune with nature, not mock it."

When Michelle opened the door to the master bedroom, his jaw dropped. There were floor-to-ceiling windows. There was hardly anywhere you could look without seeing the vast lake with its reflected trees like an upside-down Group of Seven painting.

"What was that you were saying?" Michelle teased, leading him into the lavish bathroom. "Luxury is overkill?"

The space was large. Large enough to fit the regular fixtures, plus a whirlpool tub, plus the most spectacular shower he'd ever laid eyes on. The shower door was glass. The floor and two of the four walls were made entirely of river rock. The remaining wall opposite the door was even more glass, looking out at the lake. The glass was frosted up to shoulder level so lonely boaters out on the water wouldn't get too excited each time Settlement Sarah took a shower.

Sterling counted five heads in total. The one hanging from the ceiling looked big enough to bathe an elephant. The other four were mounted on the river rock, two on each wall, and each of those fixtures had openings for four jets spraying in different directions.

Michelle was already down to her white lace skivvies when he looked over at her in amazement. Stepping through the glass shower door, she unhooked her bra and walked out of her panties. Naked and eager, she turned the sleek stainless steel handle to initiate a downpour. When she pressed the button next to it, all sixteen jets gushed with warm water. The steam was building up around the edges of the glass door already.

"What are you waiting for, mister?" she called, motioning with her hand for him to join her.

It struck him that Michelle had never seemed more elated than she did in that moment. That would soon change. Tearing off every bit of clothing, he jumped into the shower. The hard rocks felt soft against his heels. The warm water and Michelle's willing hands massaged his skin. Her lips were full, hot, ready to open up to him as she sank to her knees on the riverbed floor.

Jet streams pelted his chest from every direction as a rain shower fell on him from above. Michelle grasped his solid thighs. Her fingernails dug into his flesh. She took his cock in her mouth, sputtering and spewing the water that coursed down his body from that mega-showerhead on high. As incredible as it felt to have her lips close around his cockhead, to thrust slowly into her mouth, to pick up the pace and drive his cock past that warm wet tongue in measured beats, he didn't want her drowning down there.

"Get up, girl," he growled, grabbing under her arms to lift her up and away from his cock. She ravaged him with kisses, wrapping her arms around his neck and her legs around his waist.

Sterling was a strong man. He had strong arms and strong thighs and found no trouble keeping her suspended in midair. His thirsty cock still knew where to find her. Despite the water streaming from walls and ceiling, it knew the wettest place of all was between her legs. Better still, it knew how to get there. It surged forward, storming her cunt.

"Holy Christ!" she cried into his ear. She clung tightly to his neck like she was afraid he'd let her fall.

"You're safe," he consoled. "I've got you."

She gasped when he leaned her away from him, and she dug her nails into his flesh. He flinched at the sensation but held her safe as ever. "I've got you," he repeated, holding her at arm's length. Her ankles were entwined behind his back. "I won't let you fall, Michelle. Do you trust me?"

She seemed to search his eyes for the answer to his own question. How could she *not* trust him? They were close. Everything was good between them. But, if she did trust him, why couldn't she say so?

"You know I do," she said at last, still clinging to his shoulders.

"Good," he replied with a resolute nod. He would process the delay in her response at a more appropriate time. "Then relax, sugar. Just relax."

Her eyes focused squarely on him as her muscles turned to putty in his arms. "I'm relaxed, baby. I'm ready."

Holding her close, cock to cunt, he thrust his hips and she moaned like a woman overcome. Pressing her ankle against his glutes, she pressed her pelvis toward his. With her gentle rocking motion, Sterling increased his. Her cunt enveloped him, and her every movement milked his cock and encouraged him to pump. He was so deep inside, she cried out in that unique exclamation of pleasure that says, *Don't you dare stop now!*

He thrust upward, bending his knees and leaping cock-first into her pussy. Her body bounced away from him, her ass landing against his muscular thighs with a wet smack. Water splashed everywhere—to the sides, across their chests, even up into their mouths. Their sex reminded Sterling of an amusement park ride. It was thrilling almost to the point of being frightening, but always retained a touch of the absurd.

Water from their slapping middles jumped up to land in his eye, and suddenly he realized how worn out his arms had become. Obeying the command of his body, he said, "Time to put you down." It wasn't worth the risk of dropping her.

"Oh," Michelle whined as her feet touched rock bottom. "Already?"

"Now who's the beggar?" Sterling laughed, turning her whole body around. With her palms flat against the stone wall, Michelle was in perfect position for a thorough police search. Her man didn't have to search to find what he was looking for. Reaching around her body, he gave her tits a good squeeze.

"What's next?" she pleaded.

"This," he replied, coming at her from behind. His cock had no trouble finding the wetness of her cunt. It was right down there between the soft cheeks of her ass. Follow that valley until it gets good and wet, and you're right there.

"Right there!" she grunted, thrusting back against his hips. "Yeah, you got it, baby. Right there. That's the spot!" Her accolades would have rung out across the lake without those great windows in the way.

She inched closer to the wall, pressing her forearms against the rocks. When she leaned her forehead against her hands, Sterling took her by the hips. He moved forward with her as she stood up high on her tiptoes, poised for deep penetration. Holding tight to her hips, he gave her what she wanted. He gave it to her over and over again, and she sighed and panted and growled all the while.

"Get a load of this!" Michelle exclaimed, reaching for the showerhead to the right. "I never realized it was a handheld."

Grasping the stainless steel head, she pulled it from its cradle. Sterling promptly took it from her hand. When he held the four-jet wonder against her clit, she cooed and giggled, writhing against the currents. "Oh, that is so good. Is that good for you, baby?"

"Yeah, that's good," he whispered in her ear.

Pounding Michelle's pussy as he sprayed her clit, Sterling

grunted and moaned. As he moved the showerhead in circles around her lips and thighs, the fine flows sprayed his balls as well. The gushing warmth of the water felt incredible, and he knew he would come all the faster for it. Her body rebounded and recoiled as he thrust in her. The intensity surged, energy building in the muscles of his legs and thighs.

"Oh, baby…" Michelle cried as he let the gushing water from the jets tumble over her clit. "*Mmm-mmm-mmm!*"

Her arousal inspired his. Though she panted and moaned and begged for mercy, the water kept right on coursing at them from all directions. When an errant jet of soft, warm water caressed his balls, he just couldn't hold back. "Oh, yeah, baby girl, you do me so good, so good, *so good!*" He squeezed his woman's tits as he came inside her.

For a brief moment, he couldn't move a muscle. He was stuck in that instant of orgasmic seizure, hoping he'd never escape. His cock throbbed in her hot, wet pussy as she turned to kiss his shoulder. He found he could move after all, but only to kiss her neck.

Even after sliding the handheld back into its slot, they basked in the warm water coursing over and down and across their bodies. Even after they'd turned off the multiple heads and jets, they held their pose in the stone shower until the steam died down enough that they could look out across the lake.

"What did I tell you?" Michelle asked, tracing her fingertips across his forearm. "This is some shower."

"It's a beauty," he agreed. "I wonder how much it would cost to install one of these babies at home, parts and labor."

Stepping out to grab a pair of towels, she replied, "More than you have at your disposal, my good man."

"I *am* good, aren't I?" he said with a self-satisfied grin. As he watched her run plush terry cloth all over her skin, he asked her to dry him off, too. "I got you all nice and wet, now you get me all nice and dry."

"Come on," she laughed in response, toweling him off as well. "Let's get dressed and get out of here before somebody thinks we're breaking and entering."

Jumping out of the shower stall and into his clothes, he asked, "Well, aren't we?"

She turned to him with an incredulous expression on her face and then smiled. "Honey, did you see me break anything to get in here? I used the key."

"Girl, we are still trespassers, key or no key," he replied as they opened the bedroom door. They stepped out into the hallway and froze in their tracks under the surprised stares of four wide eyes.

A woman with crow's feet and hot pink highlights walked fearlessly toward them. Observing Michelle's dripping-wet hair, she said to her companion, "Looks like these young people had the same idea we did."

"You must be Sarah," Sterling said, amazed by her calm reaction.

The woman put her hand to her heart, stepping closer. "No, but thank you for the compliment. Some people say we could be sisters, but…"

"Sterling, these are Sarah's parents," Michelle said through gritted but smiling teeth. "Nice to see you again."

"Always a pleasure, Michelle," Sarah's dad said, inching toward Sterling with an extended hand.

"Good to meet you."

"I have to apologize," Michelle interrupted. "I had no idea you two were staying here while Sarah was away."

The parents laughed, gazing fondly at one another. "Well, Sarah doesn't know either. I'm sure she wouldn't be too happy with us if she found out. About as happy as she'd be knowing her friends were sneaking in to use her shower."

The two couples stood in the hallway considering each other. There was no need for animosity among fellow trespassers. With an infectious smile, Michelle touched the woman's arm. "It'll be our little secret."

CLEAN SLATE

Lisabet Sarai

I didn't cry until the last session.

Luisa picked up on it right away. "Should I stop? Do you need more anesthetic?"

I shook my head, the weight of my shame crushing me into the table. Tears leaked out from under my lids, closed against the hot glare of the examination light. "No, never mind. Just keep going."

"We don't have to finish today, chica. You can come back next week."

"No, forget it. Go on. I want to get it over with." It wasn't the deep burn of the laser that brought those traitorous tears. I'd endured a lot worse pain.

"Are you sure?"

I blinked in the brightness of that artificial sun, sending the moisture flying. Luisa hovered over me, an uncharacteristic frown knitting her coffee-colored brow. "I'm okay. Really." I managed a weak grin. "Don't mind me. It's just nerves." She looked unconvinced. "Please, Luisa. I promised Richard I'd be done by today."

"Whatever you say, Ally." She picked up her instrument and focused the glass cylinder on my shoulder where she'd been working before. I closed my eyes, breathing deeply as she had taught me. The heat sliced into my skin. I welcomed the pain as the punishment I deserved for losing control. Not that Luisa would condemn me. She understood.

At first, she'd been Ms. Sanchez and I'd been Ms. Wells. Now, after four months, two days a week, she was practically a member of my family. Hell, I trusted her a lot more than family. Not that she'd told me much about her life or questioned me about mine, but I'm sure she recognized the Gothic letters inscribed at the back of my neck, the designs on my knuckles and in the crook of my elbow. She was an expert. She didn't need to ask.

Those tats were long gone. For the last four weeks, Luisa had been working patiently at the image that sprawled across my right shoulder and breast. My devil woman.

I called her Lilith. She had huge tits with red-grape nipples and a glorious fat ass. Her skin was black velvet. Her pomegranate lips parted to show pointed teeth that gleamed with my natural paleness. Lilith lounged naked on my chest, luxuriant jet curls tumbling across my shoulder, the globe of her butt coinciding with the meager swell of my own tit. Lilith grasped a steel-blue sword in one hand and a hank of chain in the other. Nobody fucked with Lilith.

I remembered her birth, long hours staring at the grimy ceiling, listening to the hum of the freeway traffic above, trying not to flinch as the needle bit into my flesh. No anesthetic in that joint; I was lucky if they sterilized the needles. Not that I cared, back then. The Westwood clinic where Luisa worked was a different world. It had private rooms with spotless white walls and peach upholstery that matched the towels. One session here cost more than my old mates would see in six months, unless they pulled a job.

Richard was paying, of course. I scrunched up my eyes, forcing back the returning tears.

"Too much?" Luisa's cool hand settled on my brow. Her low, liquid voice flowed over me, soothing the hurt away. "Want a break?"

"No, no, keep on. Thanks." Luisa was probably no more than a year or two older than I was, but she had the nurturing spirit of someone far more mature. I wondered sometimes if she had kids. She would be a great mother. If it hadn't been for Luisa, this whole thing would have been even more difficult.

I was the only white girl in the gang. They let me in anyway, when they realized how angry I was and how much I could take without breaking. They saw what we had in common: my dad who hanged himself when his deals went sour, my mom who tried to drink herself to death, my brother who raped me. So what if it was in the front seat of a BMW?

They gave me my first tat when I was sixteen. I'd chosen Lilith myself a year later. She was the woman I wanted to be, voluptuous and tough and mean as hell, a predator. Not some pale, fashionably skinny blonde with tiny tits, hazel eyes and a perfect WASP nose.

Now Luisa was erasing her, dot by dot, using bullets of light to dissolve and scatter Lilith's bitchy beauty. Lilith didn't have a future. Neither did I, if I had insisted on keeping her.

"There. That should do it." Luisa switched off the chrome-circled exam light. I shivered in the suddenly cooler air. She swabbed my shoulder with a soft wipe soaked in antiseptic. My skin still numb from the anesthetic gel, I felt as though she was touching me through a layer of plastic wrap.

The damp cloth slipped down over my breast, an area Luisa had finished more than a week ago. The contrast pulled sensation into sharp focus. Tingling electricity danced across my flesh, raising goose bumps on the tan circle around my nipple. The nipple itself stood at attention, twice its normal size.

Luisa swished her wipe across that peak. Lightning arced from there to my pussy. Wetness bloomed there but did not quench the fire she had kindled. I searched her lovely dark eyes. What was going on?

Tension crackled between us. I saw raw desire flicker across her face, shattering her usual calm. My body tightened, nipples in aching knots and pussy clenched like a fist. My heart slammed against my ribs. Adrenaline coursed through me. I wanted to grab her. I wanted to run.

Then the moment passed. Her mask slipped back into position. Her ripe lips curved into a polite, professional smile. "It's finished, Ally. Come see." She snapped off her gloves, grasped my hand and pulled me to a sitting position.

No. I didn't want to look. For the last two months, Richard and I had made love in the dark, at my insistence. I had dressed in the closet, away from the mirror. I didn't want to see the changes in my body, my past evaporating week by week, dot by dot.

"That's okay," I said, reaching for my blouse. "I'll wait until the redness fades."

"Don't be afraid," said Luisa, her voice suddenly soft. "It's perfect. I don't think there will be any scarring. Please, take a look."

I heard the pain behind her words, the barely suppressed pleading. How could I be so selfish? Clearly she took pride in her work. What a silly bitch I was being, robbing her of that satisfaction!

I swallowed hard and allowed her to lead me to the full-length mirror. My eyes were screwed shut.

Luisa stood behind me. She did not release my hand. "Open your eyes, Ally," she whispered in my ear. "See how beautiful you are."

Blinding white, like a field of pure snow, my vacant skin gleamed in the tasteful recessed lighting. The skull that had winked at my navel was gone. My flat belly was a bleak expanse of unmarked flesh. The barbed wire bracelet circling my left bicep, souvenir of the half year of time I'd done—gone too. Worst of all, there was no sign of Lilith. My blunt-cut blonde hair grazed the pale shoulder where her curls had rioted. My paltry breast was no longer hidden behind her sassy buttcheeks. She had been stripped from me, leaving me bare, empty and utterly alone. And I had let it happen.

"No!" I screamed. Terror shot through me. I wanted to run but all I could do was stand there, my whole body trembling, gazing at my horrible nakedness.

"Shh," Luisa murmured. She slipped her arms around my waist and pulled me against her solid warmth. "I know...I know... It's like this sometimes. You'll get used to it."

"No..." I whimpered. I struggled for a moment, but it was futile. She held me tight. Defeated, I relaxed into her embrace. Her lab jacket was as white as my skin, but the cinnamon brown hands resting on my stomach were a welcome contrast to my paleness. I leaned back into her strength. Her breath tickled my ear.

"You've got to let go, chica," she whispered, while her hands migrated upward to cup my tits. "You've got to move on."

I watched, fascinated, as my little breasts disappeared under her palms. Her thumbs flicked at the tips and it was like she'd thrown a switch. High voltage sizzled up my spine. She ran her tongue along the edge of my earlobe. I quivered under the gentle assault, my knees weak. *Fight it*, I told myself; *hold on to the outrage. You're irrevocably damaged and it's her fault.* But I wanted to surrender, to let her soothe the pain away, if only for a little while. And I knew in my soul that I couldn't blame her for anything. There was no one to blame but myself.

She captured my nipples and rolled them back and forth like dough. She was turning up the volume, turning on the tap. Moisture poured into my cunt. *Richard wouldn't like this*, came a fleeting thought. Then she pinched them, hard, the way I've always enjoyed, and sensation smothered my concern.

"Luisa..." I moaned as she palmed my mound through my pink silk panties, yet another gift from Richard. She rested her hand on the soaked fabric, allowing the pressure to build. I squirmed in her grasp, but she held me fast while continuing to play with my nipple. Meanwhile her middle finger stroked back and forth along the line of my cleft, pressing the silk into the soft, wet depression. My inner muscles clenched and my clit throbbed, screaming for direct stimulation.

Again, she seemed to read my thoughts. She snaked her hand under the elastic and sank two fingers into my hungry cunt. Her thumb grazed the swollen nub poking through my sparse pubic curls. A pre-orgasmic shudder shook my frame. I slumped in her arms, a quivering mass of nerves, while she worked my pussy, coaxing me ever closer to the edge.

"You're so wet, chica!" she purred. I was. Her fingers slipped and slithered in my depths like eels in the ocean. "I'm wet, too. I've dreamed about this, about you. Since the first day you shed your clothing and showed me your marks, I've wanted to strip you bare and make you writhe...."

"Oh...oh...oh!" I was beyond words, though some distant corner of my mind still observed, commented, analyzed. As though impatient, she pushed the panties down around my thighs, then plunged her whole hand into my sopping pussy. I ground my clit against her knuckles and spread my legs as wide as I could. Elastic cut into my flesh, but I didn't care. I opened myself to her clever fingers, wanting more of the fierce heat she coaxed from my snow-pale body, more of the pleasure that she woke everywhere she touched.

She nipped at my shoulder, where the anesthetic had started to wear off. Pain sliced through me, a startling contrast to the sweet heaviness pooled between my thighs. I turned my head and she fastened her ripe-plum lips on mine, forcing her tongue into my mouth, still twisting my nipple and stabbing at my clit. She smelled like orange blossoms. She tasted of espresso. She pressed her pelvis against my bare ass. The starched fabric of her lab coat rasped against my cheeks. I could feel her dampness, even through the layers of cloth. I felt her want, a mirror of my own.

Somehow we ended up on the tiled floor. Under her coat, she wore tight jeans and a purple tank top without a bra. Cradling her full breasts in my pale fingers, I suckled first one taut nipple and then the other while she struggled with her pants. I ran my tongue up along the outside of one luscious mound, to the sensitive spot under her arm. She stiffened and moaned. I heard tearing fabric and understood that she was as desperate as I was.

I straddled her, pressing my lightly furred bush against her black thicket. Skin on skin, at last! My juices mingled with hers as we rubbed our mounds together. Our rich, musky scent hung heavy in the sterile room. I leaned over to capture her mouth, letting my pea-sized nipples graze her more opulent ones.

She relaxed and let me take the lead. I wanted to devour her. I had to hold myself back. I kissed her ferociously, for a long time, until I could tell she was having trouble breathing.

"Want...to...taste you...chica," she gasped when I finally released her. I could only grunt; I was too deep into my lust to speak. I nipped at her earlobe, then swung around so that my cunt was in her face. She spread me wide with trembling fingers.

The first sweep of her strong, hot tongue gathered me and drew me to the pinnacle. The second stroke pushed me off. My body took flight, arrowing up into clouds of pure pleasure, then tumbling downward to burst against her face. Everything poured out of me, the darkness and the fear and the shame, flooding her eager mouth.

I twitched for a while as she lapped at me gently. Finally, the ocean scent rising from her pussy lured me back to consciousness. I buried my face in her folds, wanting to give her the same glorious release she had drawn from me. Her moisture coated my cheeks. I could feel my own juices dripping down my thighs as I worked my tongue into her hole and flicked at her clit. She had the salty tang of a margarita. I reached around to grab her buttocks and opened her like a ripe fig, then sucked out the juicy pulp.

I could feel the tension gathering in her, could taste the imminent storm. I sucked harder, probed deeper, forgetting everything but the slick, smooth flesh I was consuming. My whole world contracted to the rosy purse of her sweet cunt.

Suddenly she clutched at me, digging her nails into my thighs. Her clit swelled against my lips. With a wail, she came hard, jerking her hips, slamming her pelvis against my mouth. I drank up the wetness that spilled from her, then planted soft, wet kisses along the insides of her thighs as her lush body gradually relaxed.

I lay quiet for a while, my ear on her plump belly, listening to her heartbeat. Strange pride blossomed in my chest. I couldn't remember the last time I had felt so good.

The shriek of my mobile broke the spell. I clambered to my feet and rummaged in my pocket. I knew who it was before I looked at the display.

"Hello, Richard."

"Hi, hon. How's it going?"

"We just finished." Guilt stabbed me in the gut. Richard was not the jealous type, but I'd told him about the women in prison. I knew he wouldn't approve.

"Great! And this is the last session, right?"

"Right." My throat tightened. The old darkness closed in on me. I hoped that he wouldn't hear it in my voice.

"I can't wait to see you." My fiancé's enthusiasm was obvious. "Shall I come pick you up on my way home from work?"

"No, that's okay. The traffic would be murder." Panic made my pulse skitter. "I'll take a cab. I'll see you at the condo in an hour or so."

"Wonderful, hon. See you then. I love you."

I flipped the phone shut and began to get dressed. My body felt stiff as wood.

"You don't have to marry him, you know." Luisa sat cross-legged on the floor, looking comfortable and unquestionably gorgeous. My cheeks grew hot. With amazing grace, she rose to her feet.

"Of course I do."

"Do you love him?" Luisa stood in front of me, strong hands on her ample hips. Her flawless skin gleamed with sweat. I could still taste her arousal on my lips. Her warm smile made me quiver inside. It struck me that, except for her shorter hair and lighter complexion, Luisa looked quite a bit like Lilith.

"Um...I think so. He saved my life. He's done so much for me." Life without Richard? I couldn't conceive of it. He'd been my rock, my anchor, for more than a year, ever since the trial.

"Gratitude is not the same thing as love, Ally."

"But I owe him so much. Just think about how much he spent for this, for you." I was blushing again, stammering, confused by Luisa's closeness, terrified by the gulf of possibility she had opened before me.

"You could pay him back. I'd help." She brushed a blonde lock out of my eyes. I thought she was going to kiss me, but she held back. "It's up to you. You're free to choose. You can leave the past behind; your life is a clean slate now. You can be whoever you want. Have whomever you want—Richard, or me, or maybe someone else entirely. But don't make your decisions out of guilt or shame or a sense of obligation."

"I don't know." I couldn't get my mind around what she was saying.

"Trust yourself. You're tough and smart. If you weren't, you wouldn't have survived. Ask yourself what you really want." Luisa had donned her lab coat over her nakedness. She handed me my clothes. "Don't you think you deserve some happiness?"

Did I? The notion was bewildering and exciting.

"I'll walk you out. Think about it, chica. What do you really want?"

She kissed me, long and hard, before she opened the door, and I thought that I knew. But she put a finger to my lips before I could speak.

"Spend some time considering your options. There's no hurry. If you want me, you know where to find me."

She seemed so confident, it was difficult not to believe her.

I slipped on the leather jacket Richard had bought for me and went out to hail a cab.

LIVE ACTION

Susan St. Aubin

D on't make eye contact," was the advice her father had given her when he'd heard she planned to move from the small town up north where she'd gone to college to take a job in the City. "You expose yourself when you look at people," he'd said. "As soon as they see your eyes, they'll know you're someone they can cheat, rob, rape. If you don't show them your eyes, you'll scare them away."

She thought he was nuts, but still she walked to the streetcar stop every morning with her eyes to the ground. Frequently she found pennies, which she picked up for luck; less often, she found dimes or quarters, three of which made carfare. Once she spied a ten-dollar bill blown against a garbage can and stuck to the side by something sticky—orange juice, maybe, or honey. Never mind, it would dry, she thought as she pried it off.

The City frightened her, the summer mornings bleak with fog, a cold wind that made her shiver in her navy blue wool suit, and the long bumpy streetcar ride downtown where the streets were full of people who seemed either crazy or angry, sometimes both. The angry people wore suits and were on their way to work, while the crazy people looked down, like she, Ellen, did, and were her competition for loose change. She found these people less scary if she imagined them nude, the angry men marching with their briefcases bumping against bare legs, their vulnerable cocks bobbling, and the crazy people's asses twitching as they shuffled along with their noses to the ground.

Neatly dressed but looking down, Ellen defined herself as both crazy and angry. She was a secretary in the personnel office of a bank. Why hadn't she applied to graduate school and become a history professor or entered a credential program to teach high school social studies? Why hadn't she even wanted to do these sensible things? She was angry that she was crazy enough to reject future careers that didn't interest her any more than this job, though they might have paid more. Sometimes she imagined being given her own dismissal letter to type, which she would do with a sense of joy, knowing she'd be set free to run on the beach three blocks from her apartment, which would be sunny and warm for the first time in the six months she'd lived there. Maybe she'd get another loan to go back to school, which she'd loved. She'd been good at being a student, attentive in classes, expert at writing papers and taking exams. The problem was, she didn't want to end up teaching.

Sometimes there was a long wait for the streetcar. The early morning avenues in this residential neighborhood were deserted, except for a few automobiles and dark-suited pedestrians, mostly men, walking to the car stop. Fog dripped from the eaves of buildings that stood in tightly packed rows, none higher than three stories, and from the spindly pine trees that lined the street. While they waited, the men read neatly folded newspapers, with occasional glances up to look for the Cyclops eye of the streetcar shining through the fog. Ellen liked to picture them naked, briefcases leaning against their hairy legs as they read. She was amazed she rarely saw the same person twice at this stop, even though she was there at 7:10 every morning.

One day, the car stop was crowded. Two more women came, the first in a snug-fitting red suit, the next in gray. They smoothed their skirts and tapped their heels while glancing at their watches. The men looked at their watches. So many people surrounded her that Ellen had to look up to avoid their eyes. That was the first time she saw the real nude man in the window of the apartment on the second floor of the building opposite, pressed full-length against the glass like a bug in a display case, his nose and lips squished, his erect cock pointed sideways, pinned between his leg and the window. A light shone from behind. He didn't move but held his arms out straight from his sides, his light brown hair skimming his shoulders.

Ellen looked down at her feet in their hundred-dollar black patent leather pumps, the heels a couple of inches higher than she was used to, a splurge she'd made the day before because all the women in her office wore heels that made their butts sway when they walked, making her feel clunky in her sensible two-inch heels. Instead of her new shoes, she still saw the naked man's image, as if it had been imprinted on her retinas. She could feel his piercing dark eyes warm her cold bones even though she'd quickly looked away. When the streetcar came, she got on, watching her feet, which were already beginning to hurt in those shoes.

Ellen developed a fascination with windows, curious about what she might see, but when her eyes left the street to look up, there were only pulled shades or scenes of ordinary life. One apartment might have a woman in jeans and a turtleneck staring out; in the window of another house, there could be an old man in a wheelchair, or a round table holding a vase of flowers. The evening ride home showed the same kinds of scenes: curtains drawn against the fog, maybe a family around a dinner table. Imagining them all naked wasn't the same.

But the man across from the car stop was there every morning in different poses: back to the window, hands on his hips, legs apart so the tip of his cock dangled between his upper thighs or bent at the waist, the cheeks of his ass flattened against the glass. Ellen watched him pose, bending, stretching, pressing himself to the window, while the others at the stop read their newspapers, or yawned, eyes closed, leaning against the shelter. When the streetcar clanged to a stop, they all got on, still reading or yawning. Only Ellen kept her eyes fixed on the second-story window until the car pulled away.

One day the man had a partner: he held hands with a woman, both of them leaning against the window, her long black hair hanging in tendrils that clung to her large breasts as she pressed them against the glass. Ellen thought surely a woman would draw the men's eyes up. She stripped them in her mind, imagined their erections rising, but still their eyes never strayed from their newspapers.

Every morning Ellen and the women she worked with brought the office to life, starting typewriters and adding machines, which clacked as they woke, then making the computers hum and the Xerox machines buzz. The building was always drafty, as though the air-conditioning instead of the heat had been on all night.

"It's so hot in here," said Jan, who sat at the desk next to Ellen's.

Ellen ignored her. Jan had no anger in her, just lots of craziness, and there were rumors that she'd be fired soon because her work wasn't up to par. Ellen envied her fate.

Next to arrive were the workers who had cubicles. They were called Personal Assistants and were a class above secretaries. Half were young men, and they all typed their own work on their computers instead of being asked to type for the bosses, except for one woman who had to ask for help with large projects because she wasn't a very fast typist, even on a computer. Although she was allowed to do this, she was much scorned by the secretaries who did what they thought should be her work. Ellen herself aspired to a cubicle job; she had in fact been told when she was hired that she was on track for one. In a year, they said. Although the work was just as boring, there was a small pay raise. And she looked forward to giving some of her typing to Jan.

At 9:30, the bosses came in, all men, all middle-aged, wearing dark suits in hues of gray, blue, or brown but never black.

Jan unbuttoned the second and third buttons of her blouse and lifted the fabric between her thumb and forefinger. "Isn't it stuffy in here?"

"Not especially," said Ellen as she fastened the brass buttons of her suit jacket. It was pointless imagining Jan naked since she was usually half undressed anyway.

One of the bosses handed Ellen a stack of employment charts and figures that needed to be typed onto triplicate forms using the typewriter. Resenting this regression into past technology, she scorned them for not putting these forms on the computer. She felt as if she was the one who was stripped, bent over her desk, being whacked on the behind with a rolled-up newspaper.

Do as I say, no matter how irrational it seems. Good girl, good dog.

She knew she could figure out how to do a spreadsheet on the computer and print out three copies, but the bosses wouldn't appreciate that, and anyway it would be too much trouble to try, so she rolled the first form into her typewriter and got to work, all the while picturing this particular boss, the Assistant Personnel Manager, who wasn't bad looking with his neat gray crew cut and firm belly, pressed nude against his office window, his erection pumping into the glass. She imagined him in the bathroom humping the floor-to-ceiling mirror. *Go fuck yourself,* she thought. She wasn't sure if the men's room had those mirrors; maybe he would be in the women's room after hours, pushing himself into the mirror, groaning, his come spreading across the glass like a white, waxy foam that he'd wipe off with paper towels until the mirror gleamed.

Later, in the women's room, Jan said, "I wonder if they watch us through these mirrors." She ran a comb through her springy red curls. "They could be two-way, you know."

Ellen, washing her hands at the sink, thought for a flash that if he could watch her, she could watch him. But a two-way mirror didn't work like that. From her side, she could only see herself. It was from the other side that someone could see what she saw in the mirror.

Jan unbuttoned her blouse. "I could take it off, give them a show," she said.

"Why would you want to?" Ellen glanced at the small mirror above the sink, then turned away to dry her hands, suddenly feeling exposed.

Jan buttoned her blouse halfway up and went out the door.

When Ellen arrived at the streetcar stop the next day, the woman was alone at the window, her nose and breasts pressed to the glass, her hair in a bun atop her head. Ellen shivered in the fog as she watched. The man came up behind the woman and put his hands on her shoulders. He bent his head to murmur in her ear, then pulled the clip from her hair, which slithered down her spine. They stepped back from the window so she could bend at the waist. The man drew close, bumping against her from behind. Ellen couldn't see what was happening, though she assumed he had entered her. It was like a porn film without close-ups, or maybe a movie in a science class for aliens: *This is how human beings reproduce. Notice how they hook together, like a train.* Ellen stared, as though staring might bring forth a more detailed view.

She thought of the office, of how the Head of Personnel liked to look at Jan when she bent over to pick up a pen or some papers she'd dropped. Ellen often watched him stare at her ass beneath her skirt, with a hint of white slip or panties if the skirt was short enough. Even dressed, Jan revealed herself. Ellen realized that she would never be fired because the quality of her work had nothing to do with the role she'd been hired to perform. Although her incompetence was an office joke, Jan played her part to perfection, just like the couple in the window.

A man standing behind Ellen at the car stop began to laugh.

"Whoa," he murmured.

She spun around until they were face-to-face, her blue eyes locked with his hazel.

"I didn't know people did that, even in the City," he said.

"Do what?" she asked. "Have sex? They do that everywhere." Her privacy had been taken away. No longer able to enjoy the show, she looked down at her shoes again, seeing an obscure and wavy image of herself in their shiny black depths. Was that her white face in multiple slices, her dark hair wound over her eyes? Wait, was that the man from the window behind her, his quivering hands reaching for her breasts? Was her body bared to the world?

"I mean, doing it so everyone can see," the man at the car stop whispered.

Ellen took two steps away from him, saying nothing.

In the office, Jan said to her, "Did you ever wonder what it would be like to date Mr. Peplow?"

He was the Head of Personnel. Ellen always preferred to think of the bosses as nameless and therefore somehow invisible.

"Never," she answered, then added, "Did you know he stares at your ass every chance he gets?"

"Yes," Jan sighed, running a hand through her hair, twirling it into curls. "I'm not uptight about that."

Ellen considered telling Jan about the drama she saw in the window every morning just to prove she wasn't all that pure and innocent either, even if she hadn't chosen to display herself in front of the bosses.

I could be in that window, she thought. *I could be exposed for anyone to see if I wanted.* She saw herself standing between the man and the woman, holding a braid of the woman's long black hair in one hand, running it down between her own legs (it was a very long braid), rubbing it back and forth until she felt her nipples tighten.

Jan said, "I know he likes me because he watches me." She wore a very short sundress with spaghetti straps and high-heeled sandals. She took a tube of lip gloss from her desk drawer and applied it to her already glistening pink lips, then pursed them gently against each other. "A woman can always tell," she said.

Ellen shivered. "It's freezing in here. How can you stand to wear that dress?"

"I'm fine," she replied, tossing the lip gloss back into her desk. "You're the one whose thermometer is out of whack."

All summer, the window drama continued. There was a blonde woman with long curls cascading down her breasts who danced while stroking herself with one hand between her thighs. The woman with long, dark hair returned to kiss and fondle the blonde, licking her body up and down until her skin gleamed in the lamplight behind them. The man jumped up and down with his companions, erect cock bouncing in time with their breasts.

One day a stranger appeared at the car stop, a muscular man with shoulder-length hair who wore jeans and a tight black long-sleeved T-shirt, a brown leather jacket slung over one shoulder. Dressed like that and with long hair, he obviously wasn't going downtown to work. It took just a couple of beats of her heart for Ellen to recognize the man from the window. She looked up at the two women in the apartment across the street kissing, their hands between each other's legs. A glance to the side revealed their partner looking up and then at Ellen, who quickly looked down at her feet, her new shoes cloudy with gray fog. When the streetcar came, everyone but him got on. Ellen looked back as the car pulled away, searching the man's deep, brown eyes, which seemed to glow with their own warm sunlight.

In the office, Jan whispered, "Don't tell anyone, but I'm having lunch with George Peplow today. We'll meet at the restaurant so no one will see us leave together. I'll have to take a bus there. Coming back, he'll drop me two blocks from the office. Isn't that wild?" Her whisper rose to a murmur before she clapped one pretty hand over her lips.

"Wild," Ellen repeated. She wondered why the nude man had been on the street, clothed. Checking out the play from the point of view of the audience? Trying to figure out why so few people actually watched? Or was he simply enjoying the show?

As she typed, she pictured what he might see from his window as he looked down on the heads of the passengers waiting for their ride to work, standing side by side in their dark suits, heads bent over their newspapers. She knew she could make them look up if she wanted. Meaningless words flowed through her fingers, unconnected with the film that ran through her head.

She's in the window, looking down instead of up, trying to catch her audience's eyes rather than avoiding them. It's the eyes that make you naked even when you're clothed. That's the danger her father warned her about, but in the window she's safe as she rubs against the glass, pressing, rolling, trying to feel that slick coolness. At first she can't feel anything because her suit gets in the way, the gold buttons clicking against the glass. She wills the people below to look at her, to strip her with their eyes, but they prefer to read their papers.

The woman in the tight, red suit is there, her butt wagging as she shifts from one high-heeled foot to the other. *Must be a secretary without aspirations,* thinks Ellen, rattling her buttons against the glass. *Like Jan. Dressing for the guys instead of like them. A fully clothed nude statue.* The other woman at the car stop wears a navy blue suit like Ellen's, with the same gold buttons. In fact, it's Ellen herself, looking up now, watching herself watch herself, like a row of mirrors flashing images back and forth.

The Ellen on the street pokes red-suit, who looks up and opens her mouth, and whatever comes out of that mouth makes the men drop their newspapers in unison. Everyone is looking up at last. Ellen feels a warm glow in her bones as she rubs her breasts against the glass and discovers she's finally naked. She looks into their eyes, one by one, stripping herself further, letting them see all the way through her skin until she both exists and doesn't. She watches their eyes penetrate her. She's invisible and yet real, rubbing against the glass. It's skin that matters, not skills; Jan knows this and Ellen finally does, too.

Her hands are between her legs now, her fingers massaging herself. She's sweating with a heat that comes from deep inside. Where is the man? Why is she alone? When will he come? More importantly, when will she come? There's a fog in her head through which a headlight glimmers, coming closer, closer, but never quite arriving. And then he's there, on his knees in front of her, his mouth moving to the hair between her legs, his breath lifting it, his tongue reaching her flesh, tickling her clit until it's button hard. The headlight finally breaks through the fog like a glaring sun that flashes on her skin. Applause ripples through the window. Did the audience actually hear her cry out and sink to the floor?

Above her head the man presses his cock to the glass, rubbing it until white foam spurts all over the window, so much of it she can't see out. She begins to lick it off in a circle, tasting fish, an ocean breeze, the fog. Below she can see that the streetcar has arrived, and everyone is getting on except the other Ellen, the Ellen on the street, who walks away in the opposite direction, toward the beach, where light is starting to glimmer along the horizon like a distant echo of the warmth she carries now within her.

CHILLY GIRL

Rachel Kramer Bussel

C hilly Girls: that was the name of the website I'd seen when I'd come into Alex's office to see if he wanted any coffee before I settled in for the night, there in bright, bold, big, orange, graffiti-like writing atop white sloping hills. Chilly, in this case, meant naked girls plopped on top of piles of snow, hence the white. I didn't see much more as his finger hovered on the cursor for just a moment before he clicked it back to his screenplay, turned to me and, with a totally straight face, said, "Can you make me a decaf?"

I'd called up to him a few moments earlier to see if he needed anything; I knew he was in the throes of it, and from earlier experience, I knew that my husband could become so stuck in his head he forgot basic life functions, like eating or sleeping. His first script had sold to an indie production company and was only now, six years later, actually finding its way to the big—or rather, medium-size—screen. His work on the second had meant that I'd slept alone many nights, only awakening when he crawled into bed at three or four or five and wrapped his tired body around me.

Now, as I went downstairs, I felt not only duped—here I'd been bringing Alex meal after meal, waiting on him basically hand and foot even though I was the one mainly responsible for bringing home the bacon—I also felt like the most boring woman alive. I wasn't jealous, just annoyed; not only had I not known my husband had a snow fetish, I didn't even know snow fetishes existed!

What did he need to look at those girls for? I hadn't felt any competition with porn when I was dating guys, but this was my husband, the man whose ring I wore 24/7, who I thought I knew almost better than he knew himself, and here he was, not even letting me know that he liked to take breaks by looking at girls making naked snow angels and doing dirty things with icicles. I'd thought we were a modern couple, the type who watched porn together, like we did the one time we'd found an old theater that was harkening back to its roots by showing *Deep Throat*. We'd sat there, hands clutching each other, while men thirty years our senior shuffled around us, furtively trying to recreate their more youthful experiences. We'd been young then, in our twenties; now, we were in our forties. Did that mean we couldn't take risks anymore? Or that if we did, we had to hide them from each other?

I looked down at my threadbare white T-shirt, the one that used to delight me because my nipples showed through, and my black and hot-pink gym shorts and immediately felt under-dressed. Maybe he was looking at those girls because he wanted the kind of woman who'd do something like that, who'd throw caution to the wind, or, in this case, the snow, instead of one who brought him coffee and made him dinner. That was all well and good, but was snow really that sexy? Not when you lived in Minneapolis and the prospect of it could threaten to ruin any plans you may so foolishly have made.

I could still recall the last snowstorm in March that had left us housebound for two days. Even after the worst of it was over, the dregs had lingered. The only upside was that we were all more appreciative of the clear roads and warm sun later. I was thrilled when it was finally summer and we had a while before we had to worry about any more storms. Who'd choose snow over sun? Yet if this was something Alex was really into, I wanted to know more. Maybe I was missing something, like the time he'd insisted I try just a dab of wasabi on my tongue, after my umpteenth order of chicken teriyaki. I'd been afraid it would sear my insides, but I'd found I liked the rush of fire to my tongue and now regularly cooked with wasabi paste.

I didn't say anything to him at first. I didn't know what to say as I absorbed this shock. I wanted to be angry, like I might be if he was cheating on me, but he wasn't, not at all. I was more curious than upset, the feeling edged with a hint of arousal. I wanted to be the kind of girl who'd do something like that—who'd do it, and like it. And the more I thought about it, the more I wanted to know exactly what it felt like: Would my skin recoil at the shock of the cold? Or would it be like those moments when I ran an ice cube along my bare neck on a hot day, or dared to pass my finger through a candle flame?

When I was alone with my trusty vibrator, the one I sometimes thought of as my diary, my therapist, my beloved, I talked to myself, playing out the scene. At first, all I could think was, *Cold, cold, cold.* Would I be facedown in the snow, my face caressing its tender blanket of whiteness, my nipples forming indentations, my backside on display? Or would he want me to make a naked snow angel, flapping my wings, snow inching its way between my legs, encasing my labia?

I kept on going, though, imagining the moment after my skin connected with the frosty flakes, when I'd settled into the snow, become one with it—and pictured Alex watching me. I imagined him holding his cock above me, jerking off, warming me with his come. That did it—I came, my body shaking even as I shivered at the phantom chill.

But how to go about telling him I wanted to do this without him thinking I'd spied on him? After all, it was sunny, the middle of August, not exactly prime snow season. So instead I waited. And practiced. Over the next month I took ice-cold showers, gradually getting used to the way the blast hit my skin. Instead of flinching away, I stood proudly, back arched, nipples bared to the blast. It was a form of masochism, to be sure, but though I'm stubborn as a mule, I also have a submissive streak. Whether in this case I was submitting to Alex or myself or nature, I wasn't sure; I just knew I wanted to do it.

I made friends with ice cubes, making sure to fish them out of my water or soda and tuck one into my mouth. Alone, the nights Alex was working late or if he wasn't around, I'd stare at myself in my full-length mirror, tracing a piece of ice that had been softened by the warmth of my hand along my neck and on down, watching the icy rivulets trail down my pale peach skin. My nipples perked up when the ice hit my areolas, and I found myself simultaneously craving the cube and fearing it. In some ways, the ice was probably more intense than the snow would be, but I felt like I was training for my own personal sexual marathon. And the more I did it, the more I liked it—plus I liked having a secret, an erotic thrill all my own.

The added bonus was that I got to know my body in a whole new way. I used to think that didn't happen once you're in your thirties, once you're married, once you've crossed some line where you assume you've done all you can when it comes to sexual experimentation. But as I gasped in pleasure while tracing a cube of ice along my labia, then pressing it inside, I knew I'd never reach that point. I could be a chilly girl—or any kind of girl I wanted. And even though it was only September, I knew I had to tell Alex, to share this discovery with him. It was hot and sexy, but it would be more fun with him.

I decided to tell him in the kitchen, a somewhat neutral zone. It was a warm day and I kept flapping the freezer door open and sticking my head inside; then I took out an ice cube and tucked it inside my bra. I kept fidgeting and finding excuses to poke my head in the freezer until Alex finally asked me what was wrong. "Well, it's hot out...and I wanted to see what it was like. You know," I said, my voice softening in what I hoped was a seductive way. I hadn't had to truly seduce anyone in so long, I didn't know if that side of me still worked. Married sex was different; we didn't need the social cues and niceties most of the time. We could go after what we wanted without (much) fear of rejection. I realized I was trembling from more than just the ice cube.

"What do you mean by that?" he asked, watching me closely. Had I let too much slip in my tone?

"I just meant...okay, look. I hate secrets and I have to tell you something. I walked into your office one day and you were looking at a site. Chilly Girls. Girls in the snow. Naked girls in the snow. It got me thinking about what that would be like. And I want to find out. With you. I want you to fuck me in the snow." That last part hadn't been part of the speech I'd rehearsed in my head, but there it was, not just the words, but the image in my head: me beneath him, my ass pressed deep into the snow while his hard, hot cock drilled into me in the way that always makes me warm all over.

Alex looked away, his face bright red. I couldn't tell if he was mad; yes, even after all these years, he's managed to maintain a poker face worthy of Lady Gaga. Then he started laughing, a little at first, then harder and harder. "April, are you serious? I just figured it was a porn thing." He sighed. "You don't have anything to be jealous about, baby. I don't really want the girls in the snow, or even a girl in the snow. It's just something fun to look at."

I didn't totally believe him. "But then how come you never said anything?"

"Well...it's private. It's what I jerk off to."

"I guess I can understand that; I have fantasies, too. I just feel like we've been growing apart, and I want us to be close again, as close as we can be. And I want it now for me, not just for you. I want to be a chilly girl. I want to see what it's like."

"You do? You aren't nervous?"

"Of course I'm nervous! But remember when we used to do all kinds of wild and crazy things? Why can't we be like that again?"

"Okay, but it's September. Where are we going to find snow?"

"We could take a trip. Or we could just...practice. With ice."

His face lit up and he grabbed me. "I have an idea. You remember Ralph? He runs that butcher shop? I bet he'd let us in the freezer."

Okay, so sex in a meat locker wasn't exactly what I'd been after, but I liked his spirit. Just then, though, he told me to lie in the bathtub and put on my face mask...only now it would be a blindfold. I lay there in the claw-foot tub we'd spent a fortune on, one I regularly dropped paperback novels in as I luxuriated in the heat of a hot bath. Now, my nipples stiffened, prepared for the opposite. I sank back against the bath pillow, letting my fingers dawdle at my breasts, lightly stroking my sex.

And then the tumbling started—the tumbling of ice cubes.

Alex poured all the ones we'd had in the freezer into the bath, then took one and traced it from the back of my neck on down. "I'm going to cover you in ice cubes. I'm going to fill this bath with them and fill your pussy with them and even shove one up your ass and let it leak out. I'm going to make you cold right down to your bones—and you're going to like it." His voice wasn't sinister, exactly, but there was a hint of danger, a dark edge that made me shiver in a new way. He lifted the mask and I looked up at him, and he leaned down and kissed me, his tongue reaching for mine. Just as I got lost in the kiss, I felt an ice cube press against the side of my neck, the equivalent of a snowball landed square on an unsuspecting bystander.

I pulled my tongue away, but I didn't protest. I'd asked for this, and as the cubes settled around me, I realized I liked it. In some ways this was more intense than a snowy mountainside, but that had never been the real point anyway. I'd wanted him to see me as the girl who'd do anything—for him. I reached for a cube and ran it against his nipple, smiling when he yelped.

Alex made me lie there and simply soak in the cold for half an hour; we didn't get the tub all the way full, but it was enough. He climbed in with me, helping me warm up as the ice water lapped against my skin. He was hard, his cock wedging itself between my legs. For a second I wondered if he'd be able to keep his erection, but I soon learned that wasn't a problem. I screamed as his cock sank into me, the heat emanating from him such a contrast to the rest of my surroundings. "Oh, god, you feel so good. I'm sorry I made you think I preferred anyone to you. You're my favorite girl in hot and cold weather." He laughed, then stopped as I shifted, hiking one foot up against the shower wall and throwing the other in the air. His hands cupped my bottom as he thrust hard into me. I focused entirely on Alex—on his gritted teeth, his light brown hair falling in his face, his firm chest and his cock, pushing into me, stretching me. I forgot for a few seconds about hot and cold, right and wrong and was simply lulled by the power of meeting him where my sex surrounded him. When I came, I clutched the edge of the tub hard, sinking back against the pillow. He pulled out and let me watch him come in the air, the liquid landing in our bath.

Alex wrapped me up in my fluffy purple robe, then made me hot chocolate with minimarshmallows and let me watch my favorite old sitcoms. He pampered me for the rest of the night, and continued to do so the rest of the week, like I'd accomplished some major feat. And maybe I had. I'd conquered my fears, my demons, my belief that those girls had something I didn't. And I was never going back.

We're planning a series of ski resort vacations, but the one I'm most looking forward to is at a resort that caters to nudists. Alex is taking his camera, and I'm continuing to practice.

STRIPPED

Clancy Nacht

'm naked and it's cold in the room. Very cold. It feels like a meat locker and for all I know, that's what it is. Hemp rope prickles my arms and I can feel it there, solid, holding me snug.

It's not just some cheap kidnapping, nothing so tacky as just being restrained. I am bound, bound head to toe by an expert, and I have been suspended from the floor.

I was not allowed to watch any of it. The first thing that he did when I answered the door to my apartment was to hold up a satin sash. It waved gently to tease my nose, and I giggled out of nervousness. I didn't know what this could mean.

John was always so mysterious, and I suppose I'd built a silly fantasy around him: who he was, what he'd be like. I read too many true crime novels, always projecting the worst that could happen to me. Still, with this gorgeous tall man, his pale skin and blue eyes, I can't help but be intrigued.

As soon as I stepped over the threshold and locked the door, he swept the sash over my eyes, leaving me blind but for the bright lights past the courtyard of my apartment complex. They were all so sleazy, those neon lights advertising strippers. It was just the sort of neighborhood that a true crime might happen in. That's why I'd moved there.

I've never had a death wish per se, but there is a certain thrill to taking really huge risks with your life. Even though I'd dated John and spoken with him, he'd never given away much about himself, seeming to prefer a long, slow courtship. I admit that I was frustrated. I'd slide my fingers between my lips, rubbing the middle one over my clit, imagining what his hands would feel like on me there. His hands were always so soft, but so cold.

One particularly adventurous night, I snuck out to the refrigerator to take an ice cube back to bed. The cold felt shocking on my cunt. I'd opened my lips up so that I could run the dripping cube between them, toyed with the hole. I'd never thought of doing it before, not before John and his long dark hair and cold hands. It tingled, cooled, brought sensations to the surface on such a fragile, hot part of my body that I almost couldn't stand it. Though I'd thought it might make my cunt go numb, it had the exact opposite effect. It made my whole body tingle, prickling with gooseflesh and sweat until I released it into myself, letting it slide slowly over the opening before finally pushing it inside of me.

It wasn't much, just a cube. It had melted down, but even the fact that it was inside of me was exciting. I supplemented my adventure with a mini–rocket vibrator. Running it over my clit again and again, I squeezed my thighs tightly, moving that sliver of ice cube inside of me, feeling it touching, feeling the cold liquid as it melted inside of me. It was amazing, thrilling, like I was being lifted off of the bed, moving to another plane of pleasure that rocked through my body, leaving me gasping. My cold fingers were on my breasts, pinching my nipples, and all I could think about was John.

John here in front of me, out in the courtyard of my apartment complex. I could hear the car horns in the street not far away. I expected him to lead me to his car, somewhere, anywhere, but he just stood there before me. I adjusted the strap on my halter dress, fidgeting with it nervously. I could feel his gaze. It made me feel small, like a child. I wanted to please him, but I didn't know how, didn't know what he wanted of me.

I turned my ankle in, balancing on a stiletto heel, feeling strangely bashful.

"I do not like that dress." John's voice seemed to carry in the whispers of the humid Houston air.

I reached for the blindfold, starting to turn. "I'll change."

"No." He was behind me, breathing heavily, arms around me as he started to unbutton my halter dress. It was yellow and flowing, girlish, maybe too girlish. I worried that he thought I was too immature to date. I hadn't known where we were going, and Houston is warm almost year round. Still, I cursed myself for such a silly choice right up until I felt his warm hands cupping me under the smocking of my dress.

The night was warm; his hands were cold. They were always so cold. But his breath in my ear was hot, and I could feel the heat of his erection behind me, pressing against my simple cotton dress. "Finish it," he whispered.

For a moment, I was at a loss as to what he wanted of me. He placed my hands on the buttons starting at the waist and I froze. "But we're outside."

"I want to see you now. I want to see you naked outside. I want to take in your beauty. I promise, we will not stay here long."

His words were persuasive, as were his hands. They'd slid down the front of my dress and under my cotton panties. They were so wet already, and I couldn't help being embarrassed. "You feel ready."

I blushed and turned my head, but as I couldn't see anything, I had nowhere to direct my blush. I merely whimpered and hoped I wasn't degrading myself by twisting around so that he would touch more than my trimmed pubis. His fingers brushed gently over my light down, and one finger slipped between the folds and out again. He brought that hand up and I could hear him sucking his finger. I was so aroused, I was shaking.

"If you want more of that," he whispered, "then take off your clothes."

It didn't take long to comply; I wasn't wearing much. The dress fell off my shoulders once his hands were out of it and I wriggled my wet panties down past my hips, where gravity took them to the stone ground. He remained silent. I was wearing nothing else, just my shoes.

When he didn't speak after a few moments, I pulled the straps of my stilettos and dropped them off of each foot and turned around.

Standing before him like this, with the slight breeze in my hair, I felt vulnerable. Anyone from the street could see through the iron gates. My neighbors could see me in the courtyard. But none of this seemed to matter, because what really made me blush and squirm was knowing that he was there. Right there, and he was seeing me. Seeing all of me.

I tried to cross my arms over my small breasts, but he took my hand gently and helped me over to where he'd parked his car.

Classical music played on his radio as I tried to find a comfortable spot on the leather. I worried about how aroused I was; I might stain his seat. He rested a hand on my thigh, stroking it absently, and whispered for me to keep still. As a reward for my obedience, he dragged his fingers over my clit, again and again. He outlined my opening, teasing each fold gently. He let his fingers slide into me and I lost control. I fell back against the seat, legs tense, arching my pelvis upward to make it easier for him to finger-fuck me.

He chuckled but indulged me, moving his fingers inside of me and curling them forward. I did most of the rest of the work as he drove. Shamelessly, I rode his thrusts on that seat, bringing my knees up onto the cushion so I could straddle his fingers and hold the top of the car.

We were at a stoplight when I came. At least, the car was stopped anyway. He could've been at a huge intersection with hundreds of people watching me this way. I'd stretched out over the seat, leaning on the dash with my head buried under my arms. I rocked against his fingers, twisting my hips to get him right where I wanted him. And I wanted him there. I wanted him to keep touching that spot. I could picture it—soft warmth around his cool hands, my body taking him, spreading open for him, engulfing his fingers as I whined and moaned and begged for more. I felt like I was going to sob before I finally came. He was expert at feeding me just a little until I thought I might go crazy or lose the feeling and then he'd start again, slowly, methodically.

I was loud when I came. I could feel how close the windshield was, but I couldn't hear anything but the soft music and my breathing. I wanted to leap into his lap and kiss him, to pull down his trousers and suck his cock. I was so aroused I didn't know what to do with myself, even after my orgasm. But he said, "Sit now. And wait."

It wasn't very long until we'd reached our destination. It felt like hours. Each time I reached to finger myself and relive what we'd just done, he took my hand and set it back on the console. When we finally arrived, I wasn't sure I could breathe from how badly I needed it.

But that was not to be. Not then.

I thought I heard a fountain and horses whinnying in the background. The grass I walked on was soft and lush, the cobbles uneven, rough. It was a suburb almost certainly, but maybe it was way out in the country.

I hadn't even told anyone I'd be gone.

The notion thrilled and frightened me, but I did nothing other than follow where his hand guided me into a room of some sort. He took me in a few more steps and then told me to put my hands down at my sides. I thought about asking what he was doing, but we'd come so far and I'd already come once. I couldn't imagine anything but a good time.

I'd never been tied up before, so I didn't know what to feel when he dragged his ropes over my body. They stung a little over my nipple but otherwise were surprisingly soft. I might have thought they were silk had he not said that they were his special hemp rope.

"I only use it for special occasions. It means much to me. You cannot buy rope like this. It has to be cured, burned on the outside and worked until it becomes soft like this. It has to be used, warmed and loved." Something about what he said quashed what little fear I had that he might be tying me up to kill me. He sounded so reverent about his ropes, and I couldn't help but feel honored that he wanted to introduce them to me.

He ran the ropes over my shoulders. It was like silk pressing along my spine, down my body. He curled the rope around a breast and then pulled it through between my legs. The rope pulled just so, reawakening whatever arousal I'd lost. I could feel the wet spot on the rope as he wound it over my body. It felt so peaceful, so relaxing to just have the rope winding around me. I didn't even notice when the rope started getting tighter, when it started to take on more thickness.

Slowly, I was being restricted. Rope was tied to rope and twisted around one part of my body and then tied over to another part. My hands could still move, so I felt the octagonal pattern around my belly button and reached down to feel a smartly tied knot of rope between my legs, just above the clit. At my discovery, he lightly pulled the rope and I felt such a gentle tugging everywhere, it made me shiver. The knot pressed against my clit, which made me moan and contort to feel it again. Ropes were bound around my small breasts, pushing all of the blood to my nipples, making them highly sensitive when John turned me around to run his tongue over them.

He always moved me, never moved around me. I was to go to him, never the other way around. His hands felt so light, his rope so strong, that soon I was completely immobilized. He bent me over, untying one section of the ropes only to secure them again behind me. Then I heard a small clatter from the tile floor. Something was being pulled toward me and again I felt that thrill of fear, the fear that something horrible might happen to me.

Instead, I heard what sounded like a ripcord and the snap of a latch. Then, slowly, I was rising up into the air. My feet left the ground and immediately I felt the hard tug of the ropes as I was suspended. The knot at my clit tightened, rubbed. The ropes massaged my breasts, held me in place, made me feel everything more keenly than I'd ever felt anything on my body.

The rope was soft, but firm, not biting into my skin, but not giving way. I was hanging from my whole body. It felt like I was flying.

I heard his zipper and the sound of clothes falling to the floor, then the snap of a condom.

His body was warm between my legs as he positioned himself behind me. I could feel the head of his prick teasing me, but I had no leverage to push back against it, to make him give me what

I'd been dying for since we met. I curled my toes and fingers and whined, trying to shift my hips.

"You really want me, don't you?" His voice sounded amused, maybe a little surprised. "Do I scare you?"

"I should be scared, but I'm not. I want this. I want you. I want you to fuck me and then I want you to fuck me again." I was drooling with it, head bowed, hair flopping around my cheeks. My whole body felt hot with embarrassment for begging, but I needed it. My cunt was twitching, begging, tightening, grasping, trying anything for friction, for more of that perfection.

"I want you, too," he whispered. I felt every inch of him slowly sliding into me. I could take all of it, wanted to keep taking all of it until I was filled with him. I tried to grab on to anything I could for leverage to push against him, but I was powerless. I couldn't do it. Instead, I had to rely on him to move, to slide his cock just there. He read me well, knowing when to squeeze my thighs, when to thrust hard and when to let up. I knew that I could've told him no at any time during this. He would have stopped. But I was glad I hadn't, glad that I could give myself to him this way, which was more than I ever would've believed of myself.

Our bodies slapped together wetly, his hands on my hips to keep me moving. I could tell he was going to come by the noises he made, by the way he moved. I focused, working with him, thinking about his cock inside of me, about me floating above the ground somewhere I didn't even know. Somewhere that there could be people, quiet people, or maybe a video camera. I didn't know who could be looking at me like this and I didn't care. All I cared about was coming, about getting off.

I couldn't remember a time when I'd ever been fucked so hard or so thoroughly. His fingers bit into my flesh as he came and I came with him, my whole body vibrating. It felt like I was having a seizure, a complete out-of-body experience. I saw stars, blinding bright, saw him standing there in front of my apartment with what looked like an innocent black scarf. Thinking of him, I came.

THE TEA PARTY

Charlotte Stein

The naked man is there again today. I know he is, because the curtains on the last cubicle of the unisex changing rooms are ominously shut. That's his sign—the one I didn't read the last time.

But I'm reading it now. It says: *there is a naked man in here, and he's waiting for you to go in and fuck his brains out.* And all right—I could be making a giant leap on that last part. Perhaps he was just in there, and all his clothes fell off. Maybe he was struggling with a particularly ill-fitting garment and lost his underpants in the process.

Everyone knows it's changing room etiquette to keep your underpants on, but it must be difficult when other clothes are wrestling you.

Though none of this explains why he was just sitting there when I opened the almost unoccupied-looking booth. Why would you sit in there, naked? Why would you leave the curtain like that, sort of dangling at one edge as though maybe it's not *really* closed. A little curtain tease, to set the libido on edge.

My libido was not on edge. I didn't mean to walk in on anyone.

But something definitely altered when I saw Naked Man.

He had that sly look. You know—the narrow-eyed, corner-of-the-mouth-tipped look of someone who spends his time doing very dirty things indeed. And then there was his hair—like something had exploded on top of his head. Crazy, possibly perverted angles, great thick hanks of it, shooting straight up and telling tales of the bed he'd just rolled out of.

It was the moustache that inspired me the most, however, that seedy, drooping, seventies-porn moustache, lying lazily over his upper lip. If his hair told tales, then this thing had given me a bible, an immense bible of sex. I had automatically imagined it pricking between my legs; tasting someone else's sweet and sour in its bristles.

He was good looking but not in a way you could think moral thoughts about. I didn't even have to get to his nudity to stop thinking moral thoughts. His face told me he was naked. His face said: *Yeah, and what of it?*

His body said: *Why, come on in! Sit down here with me. Lick me from head to toe, if you like.*

I did like. I do like. I can see him right now, slender and sinewy, arms folded to show off the pouty bulge of his biceps. Head ever so slightly cocked. Cock right out in the open and not exactly falling down on the job.

Thinking back on it now, I can't imagine how I forced myself to walk back out of the changing rooms, instead of just taking a step forward. The curtain looks ominous today, but I don't think it's ominous in the way I'm telling myself it is.

It's ominous because it's suggesting that I step forward, into licking-acres-of-taut-flesh land. I get to it, and it just stands there in front of me, plush and velvety and far too red. *It's taunting me,* I think. It knows what I want to do and fears I'm not up to it.

It's right. If I open the curtain again, that can only mean one thing—that I'm actually going to walk in and do god knows what. Even though I could be reading far too much into all of this. Even though it could be that his clothes really did just fall off. He could be a maniac—an escaped maniac from a nudist mental ward.

I grab the edge of the curtain and yank.

Of course, I expect there to be an anticlimax. He won't be there, it's all in my head and so on. Which only makes it worse when he *is* there, and he's just as naked and just as casual and sly at the same time about the whole thing.

I expect him to say my name—as though he'll just know it, through the super secret sex powers in his head—but he doesn't say anything at all. He smiles, instead, in a way that suggests he knew I'd do it all along.

But it doesn't make me want to kick him. It makes me step inside, instead, and draw the curtain closed behind myself. Very prim, very proper: I could be a saleswoman, come to show him how to check his bra size. I can even see myself passing a tape around his smooth, taut chest, letting the plastic slither and zip over his skin in a way I'm sure would feel divine.

I want to feel divine. Only in a porn-moustachioed dirty way.

When he stands up, I almost sit down. It wouldn't be hard to do, considering the amount of space in here. One step in and I'm already at the little burnished gold bench that lies beneath the mirror.

But I keep my face turned away from my reflection. I think he does, too, though he seems to have no qualms about looking at *me* in the mirror. He examines the two versions of me, inch by inch, and then when he's done he simply reaches forward and gathers up the hem of my jumper in his hands.

It's obvious what he's going to do, but I still don't expect it. My body has to operate things for me—my arms lift all by themselves as though following some forgotten echo of childhood.

I didn't have tits back then, however. Now my tits are out in the open—I didn't wear a bra, for reasons best left unsaid. I don't even really know what the reasons are at all, if I'm honest. What do I know about things like this?

I know I want to lick that feast of honey-hued skin in front of me. I think of David, always, always under the sheets. Larry, with his bedtime boxers. Me, in my pajamas and my dressing gowns and my jumpers.

He reaches around me in so practical a fashion and unzips my heavy corduroy skirt, just like that. I breathe out, and then I reach forward and lick the lovely silky curve of his throat.

He tastes nothing like I had imagined, not dirt underneath the fingernails, clothes unwashed, filthy, filthy, filthy. He tastes, instead, like candyfloss. I know he does because I get all giddy, like a kid at a carnival.

And he reins me in like one, too.

He pushes me back—not hard, but firmly—and though he doesn't explain why, I obey. I feel the wall skim my back and then my skirt hitting the ground—just knickers and shoes, now. I didn't wear any tights, either.

Everything is cold, even in the heat of the store, but cold in a good way—nipples tightening and flesh goose-pimpling and things caressing me in places long untouched. Cool air brushes against the backs of my knees. I shiver, and my clit jumps.

Usually I would think about the veins back there and the pale fat blue things on my breasts, too, especially in this light. But though these things occur to me, they don't linger. I keep thinking about my cunt, instead, and how juicy it's getting with barely a hand on me. How much I want to touch myself, right here, in the middle of this posh store. My knickers are clinging to the pouting lips of my sex; it wouldn't take much to get at the good stuff.

And yet, I wait. I wait. I wait to see how naked we can get.

He half smiles at me, that moustache quirking up, and then I see the little bulge of his tongue, running its way over his teeth, beneath his upper lip. Like he's deciding, I think, though I can't be sure until he settles on kneeling, to remove my shoes.

Of course it's the shoes, first. I don't know why I didn't guess such a thing, when I'm already in agony and he doesn't seem to mind at all. He eases them off slowly, so that every scrape of leather and slick slide of the smooth inners sizzles straight to my clit. My sex swells and grows hotter, wetter. I can feel it when I move my legs together, impatiently.

But he doesn't slide my knickers off, not yet.

Instead he stands and puts his hands on my shoulders, moves me this way and that, as though I had it completely backward and *he's* the saleswoman. He's trying to decide which bra would be best for me, just by staring intently at my tits.

Either that, or he's trying to make me come, just by staring at my tits.

"Little bit nervous, huh?" he asks, and I imagine my eyes going wide. "This your first time?"

Even if my eyes aren't as big as saucers, I think he understands that I don't in any way know how to answer that. Or understand him. "First time" as in what?

Good god, what have I gotten myself into? And if I *have* gotten myself into something, do I care?

I let out a little sob when he hooks his fingers around the elastic of my knickers and begins the slow tenderizing process of pulling them down.

I feel everything on my pussy when it's exposed to the air. I feel the whole world looking right down on it, every crisp golden hair, every peak of pink, all the slickness that has gathered from barely anything at all.

And then there're just his rough fingertips, parting those bare petals, intruding and shoving and pushing and *Oh, lord, that's nice, that's so nice. Yes, right there. Rub me there.*

He circles my clit with one slow easy thumb-stroke, patient for my pleasure but eager at the same time. I can tell he's eager, because I can feel his quick breath against my cheek, and when he slides one finger into my pussy he does so with all the urgency of a man pushing his cock in. A rough jerky slide and then bliss.

"How did you get so wet?" he asks, in this strange half-amused sort of voice, but I don't answer him. I think he's asking the wrong question. He needs to say, "How come you're already about to go off?"

Because I am. I can feel it, building tight and low in my gut and my groin. It's making my already-tense thighs tremble. My clit feels huge and swollen and I'm wetting his hand. *Harder,* I want to tell him. *Faster.* But I don't. I let him set this slow agonizing pace of in and out, the long circles around my clit and the air all over my bare body and his mouth suddenly pressing against mine.

I kiss him open-mouthed. I don't usually. Usually it's closed pecks for first dates, though what sort of first date this is, I don't know. We haven't even exchanged names, and I'm about to come in his mouth and on his hand.

"That's right," he says against my lips. "Give it up."

So I do. I shiver and shake and cream all over his busy fingers, great gluts of pleasure surging through me until I'm boneless. I have to sit down on the little bench, but he's very kind. He helps me there, as though I'm elderly. As though I've just been on a ride not designed for me, and he's been patiently showing me the ropes.

I suppose it's entirely intentional that when I do sit down his stiff cock is almost level with my face. And I want to suck it. I do. I want to swallow it right down to the root and complete this weird carnival ride of complete naked naughtiness.

But then he sits down on the bench beside me, as though we're just in here having afternoon tea. He even asks me a question that's better suited to such an activity. "Weather's turned cold early, huh?"

He has his arms folded again, as though he's just waiting for something. For someone else, maybe—his three o'clock appointment with another naked person. Perhaps he's wanting a third to join our little party in the changing room. I've succeeded in being naked in public—now it's on to threesomes for beginners.

And yet, all I reply is, "I can't believe it's snowing in November."

I don't think I've ever had a conversation like this while naked. Not even with someone I've been dating for months. Even stranger, I turn to him, as I would with a friend who I'm just having a casual conversation with.

Only friends don't usually jerk off in front of other friends.

And even though he's just done what he's done to me, and even though I'm naked and still shivering with a recent orgasm, I feel my cheeks heat. Mortification floods me. I look away, as though I shouldn't be spying on him in his most private moments.

And then I laugh when I realize what I've done and what he's done and this strange new understanding: *He doesn't care.* Of course he doesn't! He accosts strangers in changing rooms and takes all their clothes off. He provides a service of which I am sure the shop wouldn't approve: free orgasms.

What on earth is so odd and embarrassing about him giving himself one, in front of me?

Nothing, I think. The only thing that's embarrassing about it is me just sitting there without offering to return the favor. How rude of me!

"Would you like me to...?" I say, and he grins this filthy grin but answers in a way that fits the tea party.

"If you'd be so kind."

I wonder if he knows how to set all his customers at such ease. I wonder if he's as hard as he feels to my awkward hand because of the situation, or because of me, or because of some other intangible thing I can't even guess at. He must do this all the time, and yet he moans (far too loudly) and he bucks into my fist (in a way that makes me excited all over again) and when he comes, not even his own frantic hands can stop his spunk from hitting the velvet curtain.

They'll never get that stain out. Not ever. It'll be there forever, and whenever I come here I can stand in this changing room and press my face to the material and see again Naked Man's lust-filled expression and the O of his mouth as he climaxed. I'll feel his cock swelling against my grip and remember all my naked-ness. My utter nakedness.

I'm so naked that when he says, "Same time next week?" I say, "Sure."

RAPUNZEL

Jacqueline Applebee

M y ex-girlfriend, Lola, used to tell me that a woman's hair was her beauty. Lola had warm brown skin and dreads that sprouted this way and that over her head. She told me it wasn't always this way. Lola had a grandmother in Jamaica who would straighten her hair with a vicious hot comb every Saturday night, so she'd be ready for church in the morning. Lola would recount tales of having her Afro hair painfully pressed and combed without mercy as a child, which had eliminated any trace of frizz or kinkiness. When she had rebelled against her family's control, her hair was the first thing to go wild.

My own hair was naturally straight, mousy and nothing special except that it was very long. When Lola and I had become lovers, she always liked to pull on my hair, clutching it, yanking me about and generally using it to control me in a delightful way.

Lola had introduced me to her craftsman friend, Ash, months ago, and we'd been good pals ever since. He was the one who had suggested I do something special with my natural qualities. He wanted to make a flogger out of my hair; he said it would feel like nothing in this world. The idea was shocking but intriguing too. Fears of being naked up top battled with the lure of owning an item that would be completely unique.

I stood in the middle of Ash's studio between two doors. The door to the left led to his lab where he kept volatile chemicals, burners and dangerous equipment. The door to the right led outside to the yard. I knew I could leave right now, that I could slip out of the room and make some excuse later that Ash wouldn't believe. I knew he wouldn't push things if I did. I fingered a strand of my long hair and then unbuttoned my coat, submitting to my fate. I shivered, but not from the chill of the December air. Ash kept his studio reasonably warm, so I knew it was nerves that made my skin break out in goose bumps. I stepped out of my shoes and wriggled my bare toes. I was about to pull off my skirt when a loud clang made me jump. The door to Ash's lab opened. My friend poked his head around the corner.

"I'll be out in a bit." He closed the door and then reopened it a moment later. "I'll need you naked, Selma," he called out. "Everything has to come off." The door shut with a bang once more.

I folded my skirt and placed it next to the coat on a chair. I pulled my thick red sweater over my head; it made my hair fall down in disarray. I let my mane spill over my shoulders, tickle my back and flutter below my waist. Twelve years, and my hair had never seen a pair of scissors. Twelve years, and now I was about to let Ash remove it all in a single go. I could hardly imagine myself bald; without my hair, where would I hide?

My lingerie came off as I contemplated a future without my long locks. Removing my silky panties and bra left me finally naked. I still looked like a censored nude: my hair covered my breasts, my belly and the top of my groin. I stood awkwardly on the bare wooden floor, feeling somewhat like a sacrificial lamb. I rubbed the dry skin over my elbows, wishing Lola had told me where to buy her cocoa-butter moisturizer that worked wonders on my skin. I was fidgeting, and I knew it, but I was so nervous, I couldn't keep still. What if Lola had been right? If I lost my hair, became truly naked, would I become a bald, ugly hag? Would I be a freak? I took a deep, calming breath. I could do this. The reward would be worth the effort involved.

Ash came out, startling me by the speed with which he strode across the floor. He wore a long leather apron that made him look like Sweeney Todd. I shuddered at the connection and wished my mind could be still right now. Ash looked me up and down. I squirmed a little beneath his gaze, although he smiled gently at me.

"Relax, Selma."

"I am relaxed."

"I've got some restraints if you like. You can use the hand-cuffs I made last week."

"Thanks, but no thanks. I'll be fine."

Ash looked at me once more. Through the curtain of my hair I saw him nod.

"I'll make a start then." He fished into a pocket on his apron. He pulled out a large hairbrush. "Kneel."

This was something I could understand, something I was familiar with. Suddenly I didn't feel so scared. A simple order to submit was what I lived for. I folded myself down and knelt on the bare wooden floor. Ash stood behind me. He clutched a handful of my hair, pulling me back roughly. I gasped; the tug was a trigger of pleasure for me. I felt my skin flush with blood as I became aroused. My clit pulsed between my legs, hungry for sensation. I shuddered from my head right down to my toes. I leaned into Ash's grip, but he stilled my movements.

"Rapunzel," he whispered. "Let down your hair." Ash swept the brush through my locks in a series of long strokes. My hair shone and my heart sang. I was literally purring by the time I counted to fifty. As if in a fog, I heard Ash's voice above me. "Ready?" he asked.

"Yes." I bowed my head as he delved into his pocket once more. This time he held up an oversized rubber band. His hands carefully pulled and stroked my hair into a single ponytail, which he secured efficiently.

I closed my eyes and breathed out, but I refused to look at the next item Ash produced. I knew he held the shears now; I could feel the cold radiate from the metal as it neared my face. I felt like I was waiting for my turn at the guillotine in revolutionary France. My breath froze. I forced myself to swallow, to stay alive long enough to get through this. I listened to the slice of metal, the long snap of razor-sharp blades on my precious hair. *Twelve years*, I thought. Twelve years of length, of feminine beauty that everyone could see. I felt little wisps escape Ash's hands. I wriggled my nose but remained still as he worked quickly. And then I started to feel a lightness, a new weightlessness as Ash stepped away from me. A curl of warm air touched the nape of my neck as he breathed out in relief.

I watched Ash as he stood in front of me. "It should be ready in the morning." I made a move to stand, but Ash stopped me with a raised hand. "Stay there." He disappeared into his lab, only to return with a set of electric clippers. I sat in dazed shock as he dispatched the last remaining strands of my hair. The buzz of the clippers made me shake, and even when he stepped away, smiling with satisfaction, I couldn't stop trembling. He'd taken everything. Something must have shown on my face, because his smile became softer. "Stay tonight."

Ash found a blanket from one of his lockers, and then he lay with me in the middle of the floor; the feel of his clothes on my bare skin made me feel vulnerable, childlike but alive with sensation. I stopped shaking when I curled around his warm bulk. My friend stayed with me until I fell asleep.

As soon as I awoke the next morning, my hand went to my bare scalp. I felt disoriented and confused until I remembered what I had agreed to, what I had given up. Ash was nowhere to be seen.

I wrapped the blanket around me and padded to the small toilet at the side of the building. It was cold out; a wicked chill blew across my skin where the blanket didn't quite cover, but it was my bare head where I felt it the most.

Ash was in the studio when I returned. He had changed his outfit; he now wore a black utility kilt that showed off his hairy legs. "Silly thing," he scolded. "Why didn't you put your clothes back on?"

I was naked without my hair; no amount of fabric would change that. I wanted to tell Ash this interesting fact, but before I could speak, he smiled at me. "It's ready, by the way." He swept a hand from behind his back and held up my hair flogger. "The bond set really well." He twirled it over his head. "What do you think?" Ash passed the flogger to me.

I felt the blanket fall to the floor as I grasped the flogger in my outstretched hands. It was beautiful; a smooth wooden handle held twelve years of my hair that fell in a gentle sweep from the base. I was speechless.

"Would you like to try it now?"

I nodded, aware that my nipples had become erect: the small points ached with need. Ash straightened the blanket on the floor. I lay atop it, my face pressed into the warm pile.

"Rapunzel, Rapunzel," Ash sang. He thrashed down with the flogger in time with his tune. Twelve years of hair touched me, and each strand had its own stinging kiss of pain. It hurt even though it shouldn't have. It hurt a lot. Pleasure gave way to pain, but that led on to yet more pleasure. I felt a sob begin in the back of my throat as he beat me. Ash struck down again with even more force. I had nowhere to hide from his blows. I felt the blood rise to the surface of my back and bottom. My legs parted, my hips twitched. The sensation was too much. I could smell myself, the early morning scent of sweat and desire. I felt ashamed at being such a slut, but the flogger was just perfect. Lola had been right in her own way when she told me a woman's beauty was her hair. The flogger was beautiful, the feelings it stirred up within me were beautiful, and they were mighty powerful, too; I began grinding myself against the blanket, desperate for more. Now that I was truly naked, I could feel every fiber against my skin. It was an amazing experience.

I felt a thud as Ash dropped the flogger next to my face. Soon I felt the rough cotton of his kilt against my backside, the heavy prod of his erection as he rubbed himself all over me. Ash's fingers stroked over my arse and onward to my cunt, where they slipped on my wetness.

"May I?" he asked. He sounded as desperate as I felt.

"Of course." I was granting him a favor, a little something after all he had so graciously given me.

"Selma," he whispered, his voice a reverent supplication.

I felt sparks of power curl inside me from my approaching orgasm; it lifted me from the blanket on the floor. Ash whimpered as his cock moved inside my cunt; each heavy shove was a delightful heaven. I drew him in farther, sucking his power inside me, generating more until I felt like a human dynamo. When Ash came, he kissed my back all over, soothing the places that were sore and hot. I may have been flat on my face, pressed into the blanket, but at that moment, I felt like a goddess, like a temple priestess of the highest order. Ash became my devotee, a man who would worship my body no matter what it looked like, because it would always be beautiful to him.

"I think the Rapunzel flogger is a success," Ash said breathlessly. He rolled off my back to lie at my side.

I thought of other women who used hair for their power. I stroked the flogger and felt twelve years slip through my fingers. "Can we call her Delilah instead?" I asked, my voice a little rough.

"Delilah cut Samson's hair, not the other way around," Ash reminded me as he stroked his fingers over the bare skin of my head.

"But it was hair that held power. It was hair that held strength, whoever wielded it."

Ash picked up my flogger, but I took it from him and clutched it to my breasts. "This is mine now."

Ash held up both hands in a gesture of surrender. "Okay, Delilah it is."

I twirled the flogger in my hand. I smiled as twelve years of hair stroked over my skin. I may have been naked up top, but I was still in possession of my strength.

Ash reached over and ran a finger over my throat. "You're beautiful, you know that?"

"Yeah, I know."

"Good," he said with a grin. "Because naked women turn me on." His lips trailed up my bare neck, over my cheek and to the smooth skin of my scalp. I hummed with pleasure at the feeling, and then I relaxed on the blanket and let him worship me some more.

GETTING THE MESSAGE

Kay Jaybee

The living room curtains were drawn even though it was only half past two in the afternoon. Bea leaned closer to her computer to read the latest MSN message to appear on the screen.

I hope your left hand is between your legs. Is it running over that gorgeous clit?

Bea breathed deeply as she pleasured herself with one hand and typed with the other. *It is.*

Are you totally naked?

Bea replied quickly, *Yes.*

Totally?

Yes.

With her fingers still busy, Bea examined her own body. No clothes obscured the view of her pale flesh. No necklace surrounded her slim neck, and her hands and wrists were free of rings, bracelets and her watch. Her large, deep chocolate brown nipples were erect, partly from the chill of the room, but mostly from the knowledge that she was doing exactly what her lover had instructed her to.

Have you shaved?

Although she couldn't hear him, had never heard him, in Bea's imagination he was talking to her in a deep gravelly voice with a mild Irish lilt. At that moment, though, she was sure it had probably taken on a sterner tone as he repeated the question he always asked her.

Have you shaved your pussy for me?

Bea looked at the neatly trimmed wispy brown hairs that protected her mound. It had never occurred to her to shave there before this e-relationship had begun. She was damn clumsy, what if her razor slipped?

Another message appeared; it dripped urgency: *Have you???*

Bea knew she could lie. He'd never know, but somehow she couldn't bring herself to do that. It would have made a mockery of all they'd discovered together over the last few months. They'd never met, yet she'd had more orgasms and enjoyed herself more in the half hour they shared every weekday afternoon since they'd found each other, than in any previous, more tangible relationship. So Bea confessed, *No. I haven't.*

Then you are not yet truly naked, are you?

I suppose not. Bea sighed, wondering if he was cross, disappointed, or simply mildly amused. She glanced at the clock at the corner of her monitor.

I have to go to work soon.

How wet are you?

She automatically pressed her hand farther between her open legs, feeling the sticky sheen of her skin.

Very.

Good. I'm so stiff. I want to come on your breasts today.

Bea gulped against her dry throat. She could see him in her

mind so clearly, totally relaxed and naked, reclining casually in a leather chair in front of his computer, one large fist wrapped around his cock as he wrote to her.

Take a second to rub your nipples, honey, but only a second. Are they hard?

Again, she did as she was told, and a sharp shot of electric current ran from her chest to her clit, as her fingertips briefly danced across her chest.

Hard as stone. They want to feel your warm spunk.

Three months ago, Bea wouldn't have even have thought those words and certainly wouldn't have been able to write them down. Things were different now. He'd made her braver.

Pump yourself; I want to feel you come.

His reply took a little longer, and as Bea continued to play with her clit, knots of longing formed in her stomach. She imagined his climax getting nearer as their time limit approached. Her own hands moved faster as she wrote, *I'm so close, honey. SO close. Can I play with my tits again?*

You can. Fuck...

A few minutes passed, and Bea's back began to arch and her breath grew shallow, as she brought herself to orgasm just as a message popped up before her.

Bea felt pleasantly dizzy as she leaned forward to read, *Hell, babe, this just gets better and better. Did you come? Are your lips slick? Is your pussy still damp?*

Yes, yes and yes. Bea glanced again at the time. *I must go, honey. Same time tomorrow?*

Can't wait. Maybe have some sex toys to play with—oh, and I hope you'll be naked for me by then.

Bea didn't reply. She would normally have sent a final *Goodbye* message, but today she just sat staring at the PC screen as her pulse rate returned to normal. He wasn't going to let this go. He really did want her to shave, but what was the point when they never saw each other? Even as she asked herself the question, Bea knew the answer. It was power and submission. Control for him and delicious obedience for her.

Sick of relationships turning sour on her, Bea had taken the advice of a more liberated friend and investigated a few dating sites, hoping that actually having her requirements stated before any date took place would at least give any potential partner no excuse to suddenly reveal he smoked forty a day, after months of insisting he'd never smoked and that the lingering smell around him was due to a work colleague, and all such similar excuses.

After a few failed attempts, Bea had accidently come across a site specializing in casual relationships. The sheer range of requests, from one-off sex in a parking garage, to couples requiring an extra person for a threesome, and on to women seeking their first lesbian experience, both amazed and fascinated Bea. She found herself studying each one in depth, wishing she was brave enough to make the call, or write the email, that would take her into that hitherto unknown world.

Then, on her third visit to the site, she read an advert entitled, *Naked at my computer.* Intrigued, Bea had read on.

Do you have half an hour a day to sit naked at your computer? Do you want to join me for a late lunch break over the technological highway, while we message each other to climax? I'm male, 6 foot 2, have dark hair and darker eyes—the rest I'll leave to your imagination... Females only please.

Bea remembered clearly how her heart had thudded in her chest as she replied, telling herself that it was okay because they'd never meet, that it wouldn't be real, that she could back out anytime. She hadn't backed out, though; she hadn't wanted to. They'd taken it slowly, gotten to know each other, their hopes, dreams and most of all, their deepest erotic fantasies: Hers, to be told what to do. His, for her to obey him. Could she do this for him though? Could she make herself one–hundred-percent naked?

Bea manipulated her labia's secret folds, feeling the tickle of hairs beneath her touch. Since her teenage years, she had been a regular visitor to the local beauty salon, preferring to endure the pain of waxing rather than risk her clumsy fingers with a razor. There was no way she could go there for this though. She'd blush just asking.

Putting away the penultimate item from her shopping bag, Bea pulled out the pack of lady's razors and accompanying shaving gel and moisturizer with a trembling hand. "Not good," she spoke sternly to herself, "if you can't get them out of your carrier bag without your hands shaking!"

She checked her watch. It was one o'clock. That meant she had an hour and a half to do this. Bea ran a deep, warm bath, and after lining up her new equipment on the side of the tub, lowered herself into its calming depths. Her legs and underarms were already sorted from recent visits to the salon, but she'd only ever kept her pussy in order with the occasional trim from her sharp silver nail scissors.

Reading and then rereading the seemingly simple instructions on the gel tube, Bea widened her legs as far as the bath would allow and smeared the pale blue gunk over her mound. She gasped at the contrast in temperature; it was so cold, and the water lapping around her rather haphazardly as she maneuvered the gel into every nook and cranny of her pussy was comfortably warm. She was shocked at how nice it felt, at how such a mundane act had caused her nipples to tighten so obviously.

All feelings of unexpected arousal disappeared as she picked up the razor. Her clumsiness in life was a matter of record Bea could not dispute. She was always catching her arms on door frames, stubbing her toes, banging her elbows on cupboards that had stood in the same place for years.

She took a calming breath. This was ridiculous; millions of women did this every day without even a second thought, probably at speed! Taking off the razor's protective cover without cutting herself was a good start. Bea dipped the blade into the water, and then, with as steady a hand as she could manage, brought the razor to the edge of her soft, blue-gelled skin. Gently, she pulled the tool across the top of the gel, watching in morbid fascination as the creamy substance gathered up a mass of dark brown hairs in one surprisingly easy, and not unpleasant, move. Rinsing off the blade, Bea did it again, and again, and soon the easily reached areas at the top of her pussy were completely clear.

Now she had to go even slower. How was she ever going to get the razor between her lower lips and the sides of her legs? Feeling like a contortionist, Bea tilted her body so she could reach farther into her most intimate area.

Taking a new squeeze of gel, Bea rubbed the thick substance in her palm and reapplied it, kneading it slowly into her sensitive creases. A quiver of desire ran down Bea's spine. What would her lover think if he could see this? She began to relax, concentrating on how this new experience felt, so she could describe it to him later.

In her mind, Bea could see him. He stood next to the bath. Silent. Naked. Watching. His face set in an expression of satisfaction. He wasn't smiling, but she could tell he was pleased— his eyes gave him away.

The fear of cutting herself returned as the razor swiped away the few remaining hairs. Yet, despite her caution, she couldn't help but react to the cold cream and even colder metal that caressed her. Blowing out gently through her concentration-pursed lips, Bea brought the razor over her peach flesh for the final time, aware that the wetness between her legs wasn't entirely due to the bathwater.

Putting the cap carefully back on the razor, Bea washed away the remaining gel and bent forward to examine her handiwork. She ran a single digit over the newly denuded skin, making her body tighten and her tits swell. It was like looking at the nub of a stranger, like running a hand over the pussy of another woman, yet still being able to enjoy all the pleasure of the touch.

Bea pulled the plug on the bath but remained where she was as the water drained away. Taking up the small tube of after-shave lotion, Bea dispensed a pea-sized dollop into her palm and lying back with her eyes closed, began to ease it into her freshly shaved mound.

Moving slowly, Bea pictured her lover moving closer as he witnessed the skin pucker and blush beneath the smoothing cream. Once all the moisturizer had dissolved, Bea slipped her hand lower, massaging the juice that was now flowing freely from her cunt. Her stomach fluttered as the sensations she'd experienced so many times before felt more intense now that the barrier of hair between her touch and her desire had been removed.

Bending her knees, Bea pushed a finger inside herself and rubbed her clit with another, while her other hand pinched her right nipple, hard, just like she did when her lover instructed her to. Her climax was short and sweet, leaving her shivering from both relieved satisfaction and the sudden awareness of being physically cold, after staying so long in an empty bath.

Drying quickly, Bea glanced at the bedroom clock. There were only twenty minutes until she was due to email him. Deciding not to bother getting dressed, Bea put on a blue silk robe, logged onto the computer and patiently waited for half past two to arrive.

Are you naked?

Yes.

Totally naked??

Bea felt a glow of pride flow through her as she typed, *Yes, totally naked.*

The pause before the next message spoke volumes to Bea. She wondered how much firmer his shaft had gone. Was he struggling to control himself? Did he want to come right then and there and not make himself wait the full half an hour as usual?

You've shaved?

I have. It took a lot of nerve, but yes, I did it. For you.

What did it feel like?

Bea could almost feel him holding his breath.

It was weird. I'm so scared of razors. I thought it would hurt, but it didn't, and I thought I'd cut myself, but I didn't do that, either. Then, as the shaving gel soothed me, I began to use the razor, and I imagined you watching me, helping me to relax.

Did it turn you on?

Bea smiled, her gray-blue eyes lighting up as she watched her words appear on the monitor. *It did.* Feeling braver than she had in a long time, she asked him what she longed to know. *Are you hard, honey? Does the idea of my nude pussy turn you on?*

Like you have no idea! I'm like a bloody plank of wood here!

Go ahead. Start pumping. An unfamiliar thrill of control filled Bea as she took the upper hand. *My left hand is already between my legs. I can't stop stroking myself. It feels so different. So free. So wet! I'm so fucking horny!*

Hell, girl...I'm close already.

Me, too. Bea reached out to her faithful bag of sex toys and pulled out her favorite vibrator. *I have my toy bag here.*

Tell me more.

I'm taking up a blue vibrator. A BIG *blue vibrator with a bunny attachment. It's buzzing, and I'm running it over the very tip of my clit.*

Put it in.

I'd be delighted! Bea's throat dried as the toy hammered against her insides, and the small bunny ears tickled her now extra-vulnerable pussy.

The spelling on his typing showed Bea just how close her lover was as she read, *Any secnd now, I can see you, I can se u,,, Rub your titss.*

Bea felt a further hit of power wash over her, as the vibe pushed her over the edge, while her fingers played with her right nipple. Her muscles knotted, and she rocked back against her desk chair as, with legs wide, Bea let her toy maintain the climax until she could stand it no longer.

With shaking hands, Bea typed, *Fuck, that was good. I haven't come like that for a long time.*

Grinning, Bea read his response as, word by word, it appeared before her. *Babe, I just shot my load all over the carpet—no way could I make it to the bathroom in time. You are incredible! Didn't I tell you it would be better when you were totally naked?*

Bea couldn't argue with that.

IVY LEAGUE ASSOCIATES

Donna George Storey

Are you ready to move up to a new league tonight, Erica?" Jenny kept her voice confidential, although I knew she'd already hung up on the client.

"What do you mean?" I'd been lounging on her sofa like an odalisque, but now I sat up, my interest piqued. I knew my old friend had been coddling me with her easiest jobs so far.

"This client likes it kinky. But just a little." She held her thumb and forefinger about a quarter inch apart and smiled.

I smiled back. "I've done pretty well with that Viennese guy who likes to chat about Mahler and Freud for an hour, then asks me to show him my tits." Ernst had already requested me three times in two weeks. He always paid for full "executive" service even though he only gazed longingly at my naked breasts for a minute or two before he sent me home.

"I'm trying to ease you into it, darling. After all, you are my only 'associate' who's actually graduated from an Ivy League school."

"Glad I can finally make an honest woman out of you. So, what's with the kinky guy?"

"He just wants you to show up at his place wearing a raincoat. With nothing on underneath."

"You mean I have to be completely nude?"

"Wear thigh-highs and a push-up bra, the standard uniform. But skip the panties. And he'll ask you to take off the coat slowly, a little striptease. After that, it's in-and-out vanilla."

In spite of myself, I felt a twinge in my lower regions. Walking around the city commando happened to be a private indulgence of my own, but I quickly reminded myself this had nothing to do with my desire or even sex. It was all business.

The boss mistook my frown for reluctance.

"I do think you can handle it, Erica. This client gets good reports all around. He's quite good looking and, um, he knows what he's doing—or so they tell me."

"Then why does he have to call us?" The question slipped out before I could stop myself. I'd been helping Jenny out now and then for about a month, but it was already long enough to have figured out that the clichés about escort services and their patrons were mostly bullshit.

Jenny shrugged. "He's one of those Wall Street guys. Too busy mastering the universe to bother with the care and feeding of an amateur girlfriend. It's a dog's life, really. In any case, I'm sure this will be excellent material for your book."

She must have had a slim roster of "associates" on call tonight, because Jenny was really laying it on thick. "Okay, okay. Tell Mr. Wall Street I'm on my way. Bare naked from tits to thighs."

"You're a doll, Erica." She gave me an address in the West Village and had the client on her cell before I was out of my dress and panties. "Hello, it's Ivy from Ivy League Associates.

Kimberly will be there within half an hour. She's a lovely new associate, strawberry blonde, an artist and a recent graduate of Princeton...."

I had to snicker. "Ivy"—actually my former roommate back at old Nassau—purveyed sex, to be sure, but what she really sold these guys was illusion, pretty little lies. Yet, oddly enough, this time her sales pitch was absolutely true.

I almost felt sorry for that sucker on the other end of the line.

"Walk straight through the front building to the carriage house. The doors in the back are both open, so come right in." The male voice coming through the intercom was pleasantly deep but businesslike, as if he were expecting the delivery of a legal document or Chinese takeout.

The rasp of the security buzzer cut through the night, and I pushed the front door open, ignoring the queasy feeling in my stomach as I passed apartment 1A, then 1B, silent in the wee hours of a Wednesday morning. For all my nonchalance in front of "Ivy," I still experienced beginner's nerves at exactly this point every time. Nothing got to me about this unlikely employment as much as the *moment before*, when the man who would pay me to have sex with him was still faceless, an enveloping, hard-muscled body, as dark and glittering as a dream. It took all I had not to turn on my stilettos and run, but I set my jaw and sauntered through the back door into the courtyard. I'd discover soon enough that this daunting phantom of Male Power was nothing but a naked guy with a boner.

Which was something I knew how to manage with no problem at all.

Yet my steps faltered again before the façade of the cute carriage house, all whitewashed brick and glossy shutters. Pots of flowers—no doubt tended by a professional gardener—slumbered languidly in the glow of old-fashioned brass lanterns. I hadn't realized such charming places existed in secret corners of this cold, gritty city.

I rested my hand on the shiny doorknob and turned it cautiously. The door gave, as promised, and I stepped inside. The room was darker than the courtyard, and it took a moment for my eyes to adjust. Hazy shapes shifted into gray focus: a male figure in a light-colored robe lounging back on a sofa, a whiskey bottle and glass glimmering faintly in the shadows.

"Hey. Kimberly?"

It was that same investment banker voice but with a new touch of warmth.

"That's what they call me. And what would you like me to call you?"

The man laughed. "Tom will do. I hear you went to Princeton. What class?"

Something in his tone made my shoulders tense. What was with the condescension? Was this stuffed shirt a Yalie or something?

"Class of two thousand two." I instinctively stood taller.

He snorted.

"What's so funny?" I blurted out.

"I'll tell you later. Would you like something to drink, Kimberly?"

I usually accepted something out of courtesy, but our little tussle over my alma mater had put me in the mood to get on with the show—on my terms.

"No, I don't need anything to drink," I said, notching my voice down seductively. "It would feel a little strange to sip a cocktail in a raincoat with nothing on underneath."

I heard an intake of breath. *Touché.*

I continued, "Of course, it felt really strange riding over here in the cab, with the soft lining of my coat rubbing against my bare asscheeks."

Tom swallowed audibly. "Did...did you enjoy it?"

I certainly enjoyed the way his voice quivered slightly, his arrogance evaporated like dew in the sun. "Well, at first I kept worrying the driver would find out I wasn't...properly dressed. But then I started liking the sensation of the silky fabric against my skin. It even turned me on a little."

"Oh, yeah?" he breathed.

"It was kind of like a hand rubbing me back there. And as I was walking up to your front building, a breeze came along and sort of snaked up between my legs to tickle my naked pussy. It was very distracting. I've never walked around outside without panties before," I lied.

"Is that so?" he said, his voice husky. Through the gloom I noticed his hand move down to the obvious lump in his robe, just below the belt.

"I've been so busy being a good girl, going to Princeton and getting As and all that, I'd never really thought about doing something so naughty. It's almost like one of those dreams where you're at school and you realize you forgot to get dressed. So everyone sees the real you, naked and vulnerable, your private yearnings all exposed. Only a very bad girl would let people see that part of her. Fortunately no one will see my little slipup tonight—except you."

The man made a funny sound in his throat, which usually meant in about five seconds he'd be begging for my hot mouth or my slick, wet pussy. This client, however, surprised me yet again.

"You have a gift for words, Kimberly. You might consider a second career in phone sex," he observed dryly. "What did you major in at Princeton? Psychology? Or creative writing perhaps?" He stressed the word *Princeton* again in a way that made me bristle. No doubt about it—he was a fucking Yalie.

"As a matter of fact, I did major in creative writing," I said haughtily. Actually at Princeton "creative writing" was a certificate program, not a major, but he didn't deserve that information.

"The problem is I'm in the mood for some action right now. So why don't you zip your lips, unbutton your coat, and turn around and face the door?"

His patronizing brusqueness was like a slap. My belly contracted, anger mingled with an unsettling dash of lust. The guy was clearly used to giving orders. And—for better or worse—it was my job to take them.

Pressing my lips together, I pivoted away from him and quickly undid my buttons.

"Now pull the coat down slowly. I want to see that naked ass you've been advertising so eloquently."

"Yes, sir," I murmured mutinously under my breath. Maybe that's why Jenny had buttered me up with reports of his good looks and bedroom skills—the guy was an asshole, pure and simple. And yet my pulse was racing as I eased the coat over my shoulders, drew my arms from the sleeves and then inched the cloth down over my hips, letting it fall to the floor in a puddle.

A good long minute passed before he grunted his approval. "You definitely have a great ass. Now you can turn back around."

My skin felt hot and flushed even in the darkness, which was strange because I bared my breasts for old Ernst in full daylight with nary a blush. Timidly, I glanced toward the sofa. Glittering eyes leaped through the dim light, flicking up and down my body like a tongue.

I'd never felt so naked in my life.

"Come here."

I hesitated. Why was this so difficult? Jenny was right that the kink aspect was minimal. So the guy got off on the idea of chicks walking around naked under their coats. So his dick got harder when he played boss like he was still at the office. I'd already done this half a dozen times—walked straight into a stranger's embrace, let him touch me as if we actually meant something to each other. But of course we didn't, which is what kept us both safe in the end.

Squaring my shoulders, I walked over to the sofa and stood beside him, avoiding those probing eyes. A large, warm hand reached out to cup my buttock. Fingers danced over the flesh lightly, teasingly, then squeezed, almost hard enough to hurt. I stiffened.

"Hey, your skin's chilly." His voice was softer now.

"That's because you made me walk around naked at two in the morning, you idiot," I retorted.

He laughed again, but this time it was friendly. "I suppose it is my fault. Why don't you climb on my lap and I'll try to warm you up?"

"I'll admit I'm curious to see what you can do," I said saucily, back in the game. I swung a leg over him and settled just above the bulge tenting his robe. The fabric was soft, but nubby at the same time, and it chafed my tender parts in a disturbingly pleasant way.

He fingered the clasp of my push-up bra. "May I take this off, too?"

"Why so polite all of a sudden? Is it because I'm rubbing my bare cunt all over your bathrobe?"

"You're spunky. I like that," he said, his gaze fixed firmly on my tits as the clasp sprung free and the bra sagged, baring my stiff nipples.

I shimmied the bra straps down over my arms. "You might like my spunk, but will I like yours?"

I sensed a clever comeback hovering on his lips, but instead he cocked his head and studied my face as if he were seeing me for the first time. In spite of myself, I gazed back. I felt another twist of lust in my secret places, like an echo of a long-lost memory. I didn't usually go for "handsome" types, but there was definitely something about this guy. I looked away.

"Do you mind if I turn on the light?" he said. "I want to see your pretty face."

"You're the one who wanted it dark."

"I usually prefer it that way, but not tonight."

He reached over to the end table and turned on the lamp.

Blinking, our eyes met again.

We froze, our jaws sagging in mutual alarm.

"Fuck, do I know you?" "Tom" sounded even more shocked than I felt. His erection immediately wilted under me.

"I think so. You're Tyler Compton, right? From my History Three Seventy-seven precept junior year. The Gilded Age and Progressive Era."

"And you're Erica Marshall. Jeez, you weren't lying when you said you went to Princeton."

"You didn't believe me, did you?"

"These girls, they'll say anything. I only believe what they do. But yeah, hey, you look exactly the same." Ty was staring at me as if he'd found some boyhood treasure he'd forgotten.

Only then did I think to cross my arms over my exposed chest.

Suddenly the word *naked* took on a whole new meaning.

"Do you mind if I put my coat back on?" I said in a small voice.

"Oh, sure. Sorry. Let me get it for you."

He helped me up awkwardly, plucked my crumpled coat from the floor and held it for me, like an old-fashioned gentleman. Once I was decently attired, we settled back on the sofa, side by side, our shoulders hunched shyly. Call it my business sense, but I wondered, perversely, if he'd still pay me for the hour.

"Wow, well, Erica, what've you been doing with yourself? I didn't get to Reunions last spring. Work was crazy as always."

"I didn't go, either. I was out in Iowa, doing my MFA." No need to mention I hadn't finished my thesis yet and was frankly terrified I never would.

"Oh, you really are a writer? Cool. I'm an associate at Goldman Sachs."

"It looks like you're doing well," I said, gesturing around the living room that bore the sleek asceticism of a decorator's idea of manly elegance.

"I am doing well," he said with no irony. "Very well. And you, seriously, you look great. I can't believe this. I've never run into anyone I knew before."

"Me, neither," I said. "But I've only been on the job for a few weeks."

I stole another glance at his face. He was still attractive, yes, but it was a faded beauty: a hint of jowl in the cheeks, a ruddy puffiness that spoke of too many long nights and not enough exercise. Back in college, he'd been the cutest and smartest guy in the discussion section. He had the preceptor wrapped around his finger with his cogent observations about fiscal policy reform and antitrust legislation. Even though I was involved with someone else at the time, Ty and I'd had a few steamy encounters in my daydreams. And then there was that night at Cottage Club, on House-Parties Weekend, when I found myself on a packed dance floor, strange flesh closing in all around like an orgy. I was with Jason, of course, and Ty was with a tall blonde. But Ty's long body was wedged in right beside mine, and he was moving his hips with a smooth, subtle rhythm, and I pretended we were together, even though he barely glanced my way for a casual "Hi." I'd kept the memory of what might have been wrapped up among my fantasies all these years like a stolen jewel.

Ty interrupted my reverie by clearing his throat. "So, um, how did you get into this line of work, Erica?"

I laughed. "Insider Princeton connections, if you can believe it. My old roommate runs Ivy, and she's really raking it in. There's a professional reason for it, though. I'm writing a novel about an Ivy League prostitute, and I need to do hands-on research to make it authentic. Or maybe I'll write a memoir. They sell better."

"Hmm, you might consider finding your material in a more appropriate way. There are a lot of creeps out there."

Whether he went by "Tom" or "Ty," the guy sure knew how to say just the wrong thing, all the while completely unaware of what a judgmental hypocrite he was. But I didn't need to hold my famous temper any longer.

"Creeps?" I spat out. "You mean guys like you? Who not only pay women for sex, they rape the whole economy, too?"

Ty's mouth twisted into a frown. "Hey, cool it with the personal insults. I'm just concerned for you."

Concerned? I think he actually meant it. "Yeah, okay. But don't tell the Alumni Association. They might take away my diploma."

His lips lifted into a wry smile. "No worries. Under the circumstances, they'd probably take away mine, too."

Suddenly I liked him again. Which made me feel all the more embarrassed, sitting beside him huddled nude inside my Burberry.

"Well, uh, it was great seeing you again, Ty, but maybe I

should get going. I'm sure Ivy will send you another 'associate' to make up for this impromptu class reunion."

"Don't go, Erica," he said, resting a hand on my thigh. "Stay and have a drink. We can talk about old times. The Panic of Nineteen-oh-seven and things like that."

His smile was charming, but his voice had an edge of desperation. Against my better judgment, I sat down again. "I don't know, this is pretty weird."

"It is." Ty closed his hand around mine. His fingers were hot yet somehow soothing. "Listen, I've learned to trust weird things in my work. Coincidences, hunches. I think it means something that we met up like this. It's an opportunity we should take advantage of."

I narrowed my eyes suspiciously. It was indeed an opportunity for *him*, but it probably didn't occur to him that I'd be giving up any further clients for the night. And my rent was due in a week.

Ty countered with a sweet, college-boy smile. "You know I almost asked you out when we were in class together."

"Oh? Why didn't you?"

His cheeks flushed. "It was a busy semester. I was interviewing for summer internships, you know how it goes."

It's funny—I wouldn't exactly call what happened next a sympathy fuck, but at that moment, my heart opened to him. For all of his success, I realized then that Ty was in fact a poor man. But the best things in life are free, and even poor men deserve to enjoy pleasures of the flesh. And what about a woman with too many dreams and too little to show for it? I'd spent the last month making strangers' fantasies come true. Maybe it was time to think about mine.

Besides, whatever happened would surely be kick-ass material for the book.

I looked into Ty's sea green eyes and smiled. "You want to ask me out now?"

"Sure. But maybe we could stay in tonight?" He leaned over and kissed me.

I'd never kissed a client, although I'd been told some would pay extra for it. In fact, I hadn't kissed anyone in months. So Ty's lips on mine were like a time warp, taking me straight back to college, when a long, eloquent and athletic kiss was the inevitable prologue to sex, sometimes even the main performance all by itself. Back then, you could talk to a guy for hours that way, lips and tongues swirling and sliding together. Ty's kiss was like that, gentle at first, questioning, coaxing me to say I wanted him. And I did. So I parted my lips and took him deep inside, savoring the bittersweet taste of him, the liquid heat of his tongue. He drew back, smiling, then kissed me again, maddeningly slowly, until my breasts and pussy felt swollen and achy.

I let out a soft moan.

Ty pulled away again. "Let's go upstairs," he whispered, pulling me along with him.

His bedroom was as magazine slick as the floor below. In the glow of the bedside lamp, the wide bed had a crisp, seldom-used look to it. A business suit lay draped over a chair, as if hastily discarded, and a wallet, watch and keys littered the nightstand. I could tell right away he never brought his other "girls" up here. Or maybe I just hoped it.

I shed my coat and quickly stripped off the thigh-highs, too. Guys liked them, but that was work, and this was pure pleasure now. Ty shrugged off his robe and we fell onto the bed, our whole bodies kissing now, damp flesh on flesh, melting together.

Through my erotic daze, I realized that the rules of amateur sex were very different from what I'd gotten used to in the past weeks. As Kimberly, I had to be in control. But Erica always let a new man take the lead, too shy to bare her own desires to a stranger. Ty seemed happy enough to do the pleasing. First, he kissed my breasts softly, his mouth growing gradually hungrier, his fingers joining in to tweak and twist my sensitive nipples. Soon I was panting and squirming, begging him to touch me between my legs.

"Tell me how you like it," he whispered, dipping his finger between my neatly trimmed pussy lips. But in fact he needed little direction. For once, Ty was rubbing me the *right* way. Soft flicks over my distended clit, followed by patient—and admittedly skillful—strumming. All the while he murmured how beautiful and sexy I was, how lucky he was to finally have what he'd dreamed of for six long years. I was so drunk on the flattery, I almost let myself come on his hand but jerked away just in time.

"Let's make love now. I want to be on top." That's how we'd always done it when it was my own hand between my legs.

Ty grunted amiable consent and grabbed a condom from the nightstand drawer. As he rolled on the rubber, I noticed again, with a pang, that he'd definitely lost the wiry elegance of his youth. From the neck down, he could have been one of those middle-aged businessmen I serviced in the luxury hotels uptown.

But his smile was still golden as he pulled me up over him, and I found, when I closed my eyes and settled onto his thick shaft, that it was easy enough to slip back through the years to Cottage Club on that night in May, when our lives were gilded and untarnished. Ty still knew how to move with subtle finesse, his hips rocking to the beat of my music. An impressive multitasker, he took one nipple between his lips and the other between his fingers, stroking and pinching until the pain blossomed into burning pleasure. With his other hand, he began to slap my ass, not enough to hurt, but plenty hard enough to fire up my naked flesh on a chilly night.

And then I really was hurtling through time and space, shuddering and groaning and bucking into him like a crazy woman. I literally screeched as I came on his cock, my muscles milking him like a fist. Ty fingered and spanked me through the last contraction, then pulled me tight for his finish, his arms and thighs like a vise around me.

A few thrusts later, he bellowed out his own release, and I couldn't help thinking that even hopeless dreams do sometimes come true, but never quite the way you imagine.

Afterward, as we nestled in each other's arms, Ty told me about the dreams. He'd show up for a meeting at the office or a final back at school, wearing a trench coat with nothing on underneath. He'd know everyone was expecting him to take his coat off and get to work, but he couldn't, of course, and then he'd realize he was sporting a monstrous erection on top of everything. It seemed like something he should outgrow, or at least his unconscious mind should grow tired of it, but the exact same dream still troubled his nights every few weeks.

"That's why your, um, presentation earlier tonight kind of freaked me out. I never really made that connection before—with the girls in the raincoats and all. I'm sorry I got a little rude with you."

"A little rude? I was seriously convinced you'd gone to Yale."

He winced. "Ouch."

I laughed and snuggled closer.

Ty stroked my hair. "Say, listen, I have a proposal for you, Erica, and I hope you don't take it the wrong way."

My chest tightened, hope mixed with dread. With the way this night was playing out, Ty's latest surprise could go either way.

He scooted out of bed and disappeared into his walk-in

closet. He returned with a wallet-shaped pouch of pale blue silk, a souvenir of some business trip to Asia, no doubt. Sitting cross-legged beside me, he opened it and pulled out a thick wad of cash. Benjamins. Dozens of them.

"Wow, why do you keep so much money in your house?" I asked, taking my turn to be rude.

"Sometimes I don't get a chance to go to the ATM before I call someone. It's just more convenient to have a few nights' tips in reserve, you know?"

I studied the cute flowers and pagodas embroidered on the silk, unable to meet his eyes.

Ty pushed the money back into the pouch and held it out to me. "I'd like you to take it. Consider it an endowment for the arts. You can just write for a while without worrying about money."

A thousand conflicting responses swirled through my head, but none seemed to find its way to my lips.

"Don't worry about me," Ty added. "As I said, I'm doing very well."

I didn't doubt it, yet that wasn't why I hesitated. I knew the real reason men pay prostitutes is so they'll go away quietly afterward. Ty was telling me he didn't want to see me again. Foolish as it was, that made me very sad.

Then suddenly I got it. *He didn't want to see me again.* And that was a good thing. Because with this single gesture, we could both make a fresh start. No more call girls to tip for him, no more self-deluding "research" for me. Of course, taking money for sex is the worst thing a "good" woman can do in our society, but I guess I've always harbored a rebellious streak beneath my respectable exterior. And so, as if in a dream, I reached over and accepted Ty's offering.

He put his arm around me and gave me one last squeeze. "I'd

ask you to stay, but I have to get ready for a breakfast meeting in a few hours."

"I understand," I said. And I did.

Our good-bye was businesslike. I slipped into the dress and panties folded up in my shoulder bag, gave Ty a kiss and left his apartment with a naughty new secret tucked in the breast pocket of my coat.

As I pulled out my cell phone to call the car service, I noticed a rosy light creeping up from the horizon. Watching the sun rise over the East River was a pleasure known only to an elite group of New Yorkers—either the nobly industrious or the wickedly decadent. Humming to myself, I realized I wasn't sure where Ty and I stood on that continuum or where we'd be tomorrow. But at that secret and magic hour, I liked to think we possessed the power to be both at once—associates in a league all our own.

TRUE COLORS

Louisa Harte

I'm going to miss all this—furtively checking my watch while I'm at work, counting down the hours until my next intimate rendezvous with Mark.

Unfortunately, Mark's oblivious to this. To him, it's just a job.

I try not to think about this as I park the car outside his flat and climb the front steps to his door. After three sessions, my nerves are finally starting to settle, replaced with a kind of heady anticipation.

It's a shame it's the last of our scheduled meetings.

Taking a deep breath, I knock on the door. There's a moment's pause, and then the door opens.

"Hi, Kate." Mark stands in the doorway, resting his hand on the doorjamb.

I try to act casual, but there's something about him. With his glossy black hair and deep blue eyes, he's certainly striking. But it's more than that; he has a quiet energy that I find strangely attractive.

"C'mon in," he says, beckoning me inside.

I step inside and follow him down the hallway to the small front room where he works. His materials are scattered over a table, a movable mirror and a few stools by its side. I gaze at the colorful paints, brushes, sponges and cloths and feel a shiver of excitement at the memories they conjure. There's no easel or canvas—that's where I come in.

I'd never intended to do this. A few weeks ago, I saw the ad in the paper nestled among the classifieds like a dirty secret. *Model required by body artist. No experience necessary.* I'd smiled to myself as I read it. *Imagine having the nerve to do that,* I'd thought. I mean, c'mon, what kind of person responded to an ad like that?

Turns out, someone like me.

Within minutes, I had the phone in my hand and was dialing the number. The voice on the other end sounded mysterious and intriguing, and before I could talk myself out of it, I was headed round to Mark's flat.

When I arrived there, the nerves started to kick in. *What if the guy was some crazy pervert?* But I needn't have worried; Mark was completely professional. He treated me with respect and eased me in slowly by painting an intricate design on the back of my hand. I sat there and watched him work, reveling in the attention, the way he held my hand and the sensual feel of the brush against my skin. As he continued to work, I got shivers, discovering erogenous zones I never even knew existed. And by the end of the session, I was hooked.

The week after that, he painted a different design on my shoulder, but my reactions were the same—the shivers, the excitement, the pure erotic thrill of having paint applied to my skin. I masked my true feelings with my best vacant stare; I didn't want to seem unprofessional. But the third session was even better, when Mark painted an elaborate pattern over my ankle. The way the brush licked over my skin, I'd never been more turned on. I didn't wash the design off for two days; I didn't want to forget the stroke of the brush, the focused look in Mark's eyes or the way that the paint made my body feel exotic and sensual.

Although I liked to think he was doing it all for me, I knew it was for the sake of his art. We had an unspoken agreement—he gave me his time and attention and I loaned him my body. After each session concluded, he'd politely thank me, take a photo of the design and file it away in his portfolio, while I'd set off for home with a burning desire that only a good climax could solve.

"So what do you fancy this week?" Mark's voice cuts through my thoughts, bringing me back to the present.

I look over at him. "Oh, I don't know. What do you suggest?"

Mark smiles tentatively. "Here. Take a look at these. They're ideas I've been working on." He scoops up a pile of drawings from his desk and passes them to me.

I flick through the sketches, admiring the designs. He's a real genius; his artwork is so intricate and thoughtful. But then one image makes me stop.

It's not like the rest—it's a nude.

My heart thumps. Perhaps there's been some mistake. I look up sharply, but Mark has his back to me, busy puttering with his materials, with no sign that anything's amiss.

I gaze back down at the image. In it, a woman stands naked, her breasts painted with vivid purple orchids, their delicate stems snaking down over her belly and hips to a final vibrant orchid nestled at the juncture of her thighs. I suck in a breath. It's either delightfully arty or deliberately provocative. Either way, I want it. First, it was my hand, then my shoulder, then my ankle—now here's the chance to explore the uncharted territory between. "How about this one," I say quickly, before I can change my mind.

Mark turns around. He takes the image from my hands and looks down at it.

I study his face trying to gauge his reaction. *Is he pleased? Excited? Aroused?* But as usual, he gives nothing away.

"You sure?" he asks.

I nod. It's our last session and I want something memorable.

"Right. Well. If you just want to put your clothes over there..." He gestures to the stool beside me and then turns back to the table to finish sorting his materials.

"Sure." I start to unbutton my blouse, but as the fabric peels away, doubts creep into my mind. *What will Mark think of me? Of my voluptuous figure? I'm not exactly the model type. And will the colors suit me?* Being a redhead, I've always shied away from such vivid colors. Then I shake my head. I can't believe I'm worrying about things like this, when what I should be worrying about is stripping down to my birthday suit for a relative stranger. But this is art, not fantasy. And Mark's a professional. The only thing I have to worry about is my own lecherous thoughts, because I can't pretend I haven't dreamt of this, can't pretend I haven't waxed my pussy in anticipation of this very request.

With that thought, I peel off the rest of my clothes and stand there naked. "Okay, I'm ready," I say.

Mark turns around to face me. My skin tingles as he runs his gaze over my body. Suddenly, the doubts return. *Does he like what he sees?* Beneath my streamlined clothes, I can hide my ample curves out of sight, but here—naked—there's no place to hide.

But Mark simply smiles, his thoughts hidden behind those

deep blue eyes. "Great," he says. "Now, you're sure you're okay with this?"

I force a smile and nod. It's too late to back out now.

Mark gestures me over to stand beside him while he sets up his lamp. "Are you comfortable with the temperature in here?" he asks.

"I'm fine." Apart from the heated blush searing my cheeks. Still, with bright red hair and pale skin, I guess it goes with the territory.

"Right. Let's get started." Turning to the table, Mark selects a small round brush and dips it into a pot of vivid purple paint.

I've never done this before, so I'm not sure what to do. "Do you want me to stand in any particular way?" I hold my head high, trying to assume what I think is a good model posture.

"You're fine as you are," Mark says. "Just relax." He pulls up a stool and sits down in front of me. With his face inches from my breasts, that's easier said than done. Still, I relax my shoulders and rest my hands by my sides.

Mark turns his attention to my left breast to begin outlining the first orchid. I flinch as the brush touches my skin. At first it tickles and I fight the urge to giggle. But the feeling soon passes, replaced by excitement at the provocative feel of the bristles gliding over my skin. It feels so seductive.

Just as I think I've gotten used to the sensations, Mark turns to my right breast to outline the second orchid. I suck in my breath and pretend everything's fine, while my skin prickles and my legs start to tremble. I glance down at Mark to see if he's noticed. But he seems oblivious, absorbed in his work, his brows pinched, his lips pressed tight in concentration.

As I watch him work, I wonder what makes him tick. It's Friday night and he's holed up in his flat painting. Hasn't he got anything better to do? Still, who am I to talk? It seems the best thing I've got to do on a Friday night is answer strange ads in the paper. But, I'm glad I did—if I hadn't, I'd have missed out on this surprisingly erotic experience.

Satisfied with his efforts, Mark gets up to hunt for a larger brush. I use the opportunity to release the breath I've been holding. My pulse is racing. Suddenly the room feels warmer, the lighting more intimate and focused.

Loading the brush with purple paint, Mark sits down on the stool and turns back to face me. There's a delicious pause, and then he presses the brush to my breast. He swirls it over my skin, filling in the outline of the petals with the vibrantly colored paint. I bite back a sigh. It feels deliciously naughty. Starting naked and being "clothed" in paint gives me a kinky thrill.

Mark continues to stroke the soft-bristle brush over my breast. My nipples harden. I gaze down at them, embarrassed—surely Mark can see my reactions? But he must be used to it; he must see it all the time. "So have you done this before?" I ask, trying to sound casual.

Mark lifts his head. An enigmatic smile crosses his lips. "No. Actually, you're the first."

"Oh." A burst of heat settles low in my belly. I'm surprised at the pleasure his admission gives me.

Mark gets up to switch brushes. Selecting a short flat brush, he coats the bristles in bright white paint and settles back down in front of me. "Now for the buds," he murmurs.

My nipples tighten further in anticipation. *Does he know how horny that sounds?*

Mark dabs a splotch of white paint over each nipple. Then, focusing intently, he swirls the bristles to spread the paint over the tips. I swallow as he repeatedly dabs at each nipple. I wonder if he's trying to perfect his art or if he's deliberately trying to tease me. Either way, the sharp strokes of the brush are driving me crazy. I close my eyes and imagine it's chocolate body paint and he's going to lick it off. A smile crosses my lips at the image, and I almost sigh in appreciation. But these thoughts don't help my concentration, and I give myself a mental shake and open my eyes. I need to focus on the artistry, the beauty, the cleverness— anything to distract myself from my lustful thoughts. But with each dab of the brush over my nipples, the feelings intensify. It's like a long, drawn-out tease.

I catch a glimpse of myself in the mirror, but that only makes things worse. My breasts look fuller, larger somehow. The purple paint covers them like two greedy hands, and my nipples are bright and hard like they've been teased and rubbed between competent fingers. Seeing Mark sitting on the stool, his head practically buried between my breasts, is the icing on the cake. And like a flower, I feel my own nectar begin to trickle down my thigh...

I lift my hand to my forehead and swipe at the beads of sweat.

Mark glances up at me. "You okay?" he asks. "Want a break?"

"No, I'm fine," I say, a little too quickly, too breathless. Despite the pleasant torture, I don't want him to stop.

"You're doing great." Mark's voice sounds slightly husky and I study his face, trying to read his expression, but he shifts his gaze back to his work before I can do so.

Having finished the "buds," Mark turns to the table to select a wide flat-bristle brush. He swirls it around on his palette, making a deep green color, then he loads up the brush and turns back to face me. Pushing aside the stool, he kneels down in front of me. His face is inches from my navel. He's so close I can almost feel his breath on my skin. He holds the brush just under my breasts and then arcs it down over my belly, leaving a wide sweep of color, and a trail shivers in its wake. Little explosions ignite over my skin as he paints the elegant stems coiling out toward my hips. The strokes of wet paint are like a tongue licking over my flesh, and I'm grateful for the paint as it covers the spreading blush on my skin.

But nothing can cover the reactions between my thighs. My pussy pouts, hungry for cock, and my clit hardens, wanting Mark's eager attention. *Surely he can see?* But if he does, he gives no indication. Instead, his brows remain pinched, his gaze focused on his art. He reaches for another brush, and I bite my lip and utter a silent prayer. I'm going to need all the resolve I can muster for the next bit—the pièce de résistance—the flower over my crotch.

If him painting my breasts and my belly was a turn-on, him painting my pussy is worse. I hold my breath and stare up at the ceiling as Mark kneels in front of me, outlining the orchid over my mound. I never knew my shaved pussy would feel so sensitive being painted and stroked by some gorgeous guy. As he fills in the outline and paints in the bud, I fight to keep my composure, but all I really want to do is thrust myself into Mark's face and make him lick every damn drop of cream from my pussy. But of course I can't. So I stand there, doing my best statue impression while every stroke of the brush coaxes more juice from my sex.

Mark lays down the brush and gets to his feet. "Great," he says. "Now for the final touches...."

And, oh, god, he means it. Gone are the soft-bristle brushes—now it's the hands-on approach. Turning to his palette, he coats his hands in sticky paint and then dabs and sweeps his fingers over my body, filling in details. It's excruciating. My body thrums, coiling toward a release I can't give it.

"There, all done." Mark wipes his hands on his pants and before I can move, he grabs his camera and takes the customary photo. Then he stands back and appraises me. His expression is masked, while I stand here a quivering wreck, buzzing with the most unintentionally intense two hours of foreplay I've experienced in my life. Now all I want is to be fondled or fucked—anything to end this unbearable state of arousal.

"What do you think?" Mark asks. He turns the mirror full on to face me.

I flick my gaze to the mirror. My reflection gazes back at me, awash with purple, green and white paint. I gasp—the body I was so conscious of earlier now brims with color and life. The orchids give me a touch of decadent elegance. Mark hasn't covered me at all; instead he's brought the *real me* to the surface—all vivid and womanly and horny. *Surely he must see? Surely?*

I shift my gaze to Mark. Then I notice something—a different look in his eyes. They seem hungry and alive. Moving my gaze lower, I see the outline of his cock pressing hard against the front of his pants. "So what do *you* think?" I ask tentatively.

Mark meets my gaze. "I think you're gorgeous...."

And then I realize. He's not talking about art —he's talking about me. My heart races. This is the moment when the boundaries are questioned. I could leave and go home, but the look in Mark's eyes suggests there may be more fun to be had here. But like the professional he is, Mark seems unable to make a move. So I make the move for him. "Want a closer look?" My voice comes out like a whisper.

The look in Mark's eyes darkens. Slowly, he moves toward me. Standing opposite, he trails his hands over my body, exploring my breasts, my belly, my mound. I moan and grind my pussy over his thigh. My teased and sensitized body just wants to rub up against him.

Mark looks down at my juices covering his pants. Then, he

smiles. It's as if a new passion is unleashed in him. He tears off his shirt and pulls me against him. With his back to the table, he reaches behind him to grab a large clean brush. I think he's going to apply more paint, but then he slides the brush between my thighs and rubs it over my pussy. I whimper and writhe shamelessly against the bristles, reveling in the horny sensation. But after a few teasing strokes, Mark pulls the brush away. With a dark smile, he pushes the smooth rounded end of the brush into my cunt. If there was a softness and gentility to his artwork, in his lust there is something more primal. And I love it. My pussy clenches greedily around the end of the brush, wanting more.

Mark curls his hand around my neck and brings my mouth to his. He kisses me hard, simultaneously working the brush into my pussy. I can't get enough of it. I push back against him, driving the brush deeper. Mark rocks back against the table, sending paint pots clattering to the floor. Colors pool in a rainbow at our feet.

Withdrawing the brush, Mark tosses it onto the table and replaces the void with his fingers. One, two, three, he probes them in, enjoying the look on my face as he gives me what *I* want. What *he* wants. He rubs my clit with his thumb. The orgasm claws at me. I clutch at his shoulders, my legs suddenly weak. As if sensing this, Mark lowers me down onto the floor.

I lie back in the pool of paint, spreading my arms and legs in abandon. I feel like an exotic flower in a pool of color. Mark groans at the sight. With feverish urgency, he tears open his pants. His thick, swollen cock strains through the opening in his boxers. *I want it.* And like a flower I open for him, inviting him in.

Mark tugs off his pants and boxers and gets down on the floor. Kneeling between my spread thighs, he presses his cock against my entrance. I tilt my hips up at him. "What are you waiting for...?"

Mark drives his cock inside me. I groan. I can barely restrain myself as he thrusts into my cunt. The tickly brush of his pubes over my shaved pussy adds an extra thrill. Boy, this was *so* worth the wait. Feeling emboldened, I want a piece of the action. I slide out from under him and push Mark back onto the paint-splattered floor. Straddling his thighs, I sink down onto his cock, filling my pussy with every thick inch of him. *God, he feels good.* I thrust faster, driving that huge cock up inside me.

Mark gazes up at me as I fuck him. He squeezes my breasts, working paint onto his hands, his fingers. I lie down over him, spreading paint over his chest, making my own lusty creation on his skin. I love the feeling of our bodies rubbing together, all slippery and sensual. Mark slides his hand between my thighs, and I raise myself up off his chest to let him play with my clit. I close my eyes; I know I'm close. My pussy starts to pulse. Tiny sensations ripple out through my body—*I'm coming. Oh, god, I'm coming.* Mark holds me close as I shudder against him, my pussy contracting around his cock in the most intense orgasm I've had in ages. Within moments, Mark's guttural groan tells me I've taken him with me.

I lie still against his chest, listening to the sound of his breathing. Slowly I sit up. "So I guess that's the end of our sessions..." I attempt a joke, but it doesn't feel funny. I gaze down at my painted body; it looks so flushed and alive. *I like who I'm becoming, who I am when I'm with him.*

Mark trails his hands in the wet paint. "Listen, Kate, I know I said this was only for four sessions, but I was thinking..." He looks up at me shyly. "Did you want to be my model—you know, full time?"

I tilt my head to look at him. "Are you serious?"

"Well...I thought that seeing as we're both free..." Mark continues to trail his fingers in the paint self-consciously.

I look down at him and smile. Suddenly the future just got a whole lot more colorful.

ABOUT THE AUTHORS

JACQUELINE APPLEBEE (writing-in-shadows.co.uk) breaks down barriers with smut. Jacqueline's stories have appeared in various anthologies and websites, including Clean Sheets, *Best Women's Erotica, Best Lesbian Erotica, Where the Girls Are* and *Girl Crazy*.

ANGELA CAPERTON's eclectic erotica spans many genres, including romance, horror, fantasy and what she calls contemporary with a twist. Look for her stories published with Cleis, Circlet Press, Drollerie Press, eXtasy Books and in the indie magazine, *Out of the Gutter*. Visit Angela at blog.angelacaperton.com.

HEIDI CHAMPA's work appears in numerous anthologies including *Best Women's Erotica 2010, Frenzy* and *Playing With Fire*. She has also steamed up the pages of *Bust* magazine. If you prefer your erotica in electronic form, she can be found at Clean Sheets, Ravenous Romance, Oysters and Chocolate, and the

Erotic Woman. Find her online at heidichampa.blogspot.com.

ELIZABETH COLDWELL's short stories have appeared in numerous anthologies including *Spanked, Bottoms Up, Do Not Disturb* and *Yes, Sir.*

K. D. GRACE lives in England with her husband. She is passionate about nature, writing and sex—not necessarily in that order. She enjoys Chinese martial arts, long, thought-provoking walks and extreme vegetable gardening. Her novel, *The Initiation of Ms. Holly,* was published in 2010 by Xcite Books.

ANIKA GUPTA grew up on the East Coast but moved to India in 2009 to work as a journalist. Her articles have appeared in numerous magazines and newspapers in India and the United States. She recently started writing erotica.

LOUISA HARTE's (louisaharte.com) erotic fiction appears in the Cleis Press anthologies *Best Women's Erotica 2010* and *Fairy Tale Lust.* Currently living in New Zealand, she finds inspiration from many places, including her thoughts, dreams and fantasies.

KAY JAYBEE wrote the erotic anthology *The Collector,* is a regular contributor to the website Oysters and Chocolate, and has a number of stories published in books from Cleis Press, Black Lace, Xcite Books, Mammoth Books and Penguin. Find out more at kayjaybee.me.uk.

CLANCY NACHT is a writer residing in Austin, Texas, with her husband and three rescue cats. *The Night Caller,* a homo-erotic thriller, is her first published novel.

JENNIFER PETERS is the associate editor of *Penthouse Forum* and *Girls of Penthouse* magazines and a contributing editor to *Penthouse*. Her work has appeared in several places under numerous names, but her bylines in *Penthouse* and *Forum* are her favorites.

GISELLE RENARDE is a proud Canadian, supporter of the arts and activist for women's and LGBT rights. For information on Giselle and her work, visit her website at eewebs.com/gisellerenarde.

Erotica by **TERESA NOELLE ROBERTS** has appeared in *Spanked; Bottoms Up; Dirty Girls; The Sweetest Kiss: Ravishing Vampire Erotica, Sweet Love: Erotic Fantasies for Couples* and many other anthologies with titles that make her mother blush. She also writes erotic romance for Samhain and Phaze.

LISABET SARAI has published six erotic novels, two short-story collections and dozens of individual tales. She also edits the single-author charity series Coming Together Presents and reviews erotica for Erotica Readers and Writers Association and Erotica Revealed. Visit Lisabet online at Lisabet's Fantasy Factory (lisabetsarai.com).

MOLLY SLATE, twenty-two, is originally from Detroit, Michigan. She received her BA from New York University, where she studied creative writing and political theory.

SUZANNE V. SLATE is a librarian who lives in the Boston area with her longtime lover. She has published a variety of nonfiction articles and a book, and has recently begun writing fiction.

SUSAN ST. AUBIN's work has been published in *Herotica, Best American Erotica, Best Women's Erotica, Best Lesbian Erotica* and many other journals and anthologies, as well as online at Clean Sheets. Recent publications include *Lust*, edited by Violet Blue; *Peep Show*, edited by Rachel Kramer Bussel and *The Mammoth Book of Threesomes and Moresomes*, edited by Linda Alvarez.

CHARLOTTE STEIN has published a number of stories in various erotic anthologies, including *Sexy Little Numbers*, from Black Lace. Her own collection of short stories, *The Things That Make Me Give In*, is out now, and her first novella, *Waiting In Vain*, was released from Total-E-Bound in December 2009. themightycharlottestein.blogspot.com.

DONNA GEORGE STOREY is the author of *Amorous Woman*, a steamy, semiautobiographical tale of an American woman's love affair with Japan. Her short fiction has appeared in numerous journals and anthologies including *Peep Show*, *Penthouse* and *Best: A Book of Best New Erotica*. Read more of her work at DonnaGeorgeStorey.com.

ABOUT THE EDITOR

RACHEL KRAMER BUSSEL (rachelkramerbussel.com) is a New York–based author, editor and blogger. She has edited over thirty books of erotica, including *Fast Girls; Orgasmic; Peep Show; Bottoms Up; Spanked; Naughty Spanking Stories from A to Z 1* and *2; The Mile High Club; Do Not Disturb; Tasting Him; Tasting Her; Please, Sir; Please, Ma'am; Yes, Sir; Yes, Ma'am; He's on Top; She's on Top; Caught Looking* and *Hide and Seek*, among others. She is the winner of three IPPY (Independent Publisher) Awards. Her work has been published in over one hundred anthologies, including *Best American Erotica 2004* and *2006*, Zane's *Chocolate Flava 2* and *Purple Panties, Everything You Know About Sex Is Wrong, Single State of the Union* and *Desire: Women Write About Wanting*. She serves as senior editor at *Penthouse Variations* and is a sex columnist for SexIs Magazine.

Rachel has written for *AVN, Bust*, Clean Sheets, *Cosmopolitan, Curve*, the Daily Beast, Fresh Yarn, the Frisky, Gothamist,

Huffington Post, Mediabistro, *Newsday*, *New York Post*, *Penthouse*, *Playgirl*, *Radar*, *San Francisco Chronicle*, *Tango*, *Time Out New York*, the *Village Voice* and *Zink*, among others. She has appeared on "The Martha Stewart Show," "The Berman and Berman Show," NY1 and Showtime's "Family Business." She has hosted In the Flesh Erotic Reading Series (inthefleshreadingseries.com) since October 2005, which has featured everyone from Susie Bright to Zane, and about which the *New York Times*'s *UrbanEye* newsletter said, she "welcomes eroticism of all stripes, spots and textures." She blogs at lustylady.blogspot.com. Visit the official *Smooth* blog at smoothbook.wordpress.com.

More from Rachel Kramer Bussel

Buy 4 books,
Get 1 *FREE**

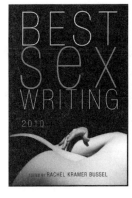

Best Sex Writing 2010
Edited by Rachel Kramer Bussel

The erotic elements of *Twilight*, scary sex laws, the future of sex ed, the science behind penis size, a cheating wife's defense of her affair, and much more make it under the covers of *Best Sex Writing 2010*.
ISBN 978-1-57344-421-7 $15.95

Please, Sir
Erotic Stories of Female Submission
Edited by Rachel Kramer Bussel

These 22 kinky stories celebrate the thrill of submission by women who know exactly what they want.
ISBN 978-1-57344-389-0 $14.95

Please, Ma'am
Erotic Stories of Male Submission
Edited by Rachel Kramer Bussel

Bestselling erotica editor Rachel Kramer Bussel has gathered today's best erotic tales of men who crave the cruel intentions of a powerful woman.
ISBN 978-1-57344-388-3 $14.95

Fast Girls
Erotica for Women
Edited by Rachel Kramer Bussel

Fast Girls celebrates the girl with a reputation, the girl who goes all the way, and the girl who doesn't know how to say "no."
ISBN 978-1-57344-384-5 $14.95

Do Not Disturb
Hotel Sex Stories
Edited by Rachel Kramer Bussel

Do Not Disturb delivers a delicious array of hotel hook-ups where it seems like anything can happen—and quite often does.
ISBN 978-1-57344-344-9 $14.95

Ordering is easy! Call us toll free or fax us to place your MC/VISA order.
You can also mail the order form below with payment to:
Cleis Press, 2246 Sixth St., Berkeley, CA 94710.

ORDER FORM

QTY	TITLE	PRICE
————	————————————————————————	————
————	————————————————————————	————
————	————————————————————————	————
————	————————————————————————	————
————	————————————————————————	————
————	————————————————————————	————
————	————————————————————————	————

SUBTOTAL _____

SHIPPING _____

SALES TAX _____

TOTAL _____

Add $3.95 postage/handling for the first book ordered and $1.00 for each additional book. Outside North America, please contact us for shipping rates. California residents add 9.75% sales tax. Payment in U.S. dollars only.

* Free book of equal or lesser value. Shipping and applicable sales tax extra.

Cleis Press • Phone: (800) 780-2279 • Fax: 510-845-8001
orders@cleispress.com • www.cleispress.com
You'll find more great books on our website

Follow us on Twitter @cleispress • Friend/fan us on Facebook